Scrooge and the Question of God's Existence

Steve Luhring

DEDICATION

This book is dedicated to those dealing with doubts about God.

CONTENTS

ACKNOWLEDGMENTS

Thank you to Dr. Paul Maier, Dr. Elisabeth Wolfe, Beth Chinery, Jim Chinery, Les Stobbe, Angela Smith, Dr. Ken Feinauer, Rev. Ron Farah, Tom Gender, and Melinda Penner for their feedback and support in the creation of this book. Thank you to Stephen Hargash for his inspired illustrations. Thank you to my wife, Maria, for her love and support, always.

FOREWORD

Why did Charles Dickens' A Christmas Carol become not only a perennial international best-seller but a Yuletide classic that never bores anyone despite its familiarity? In whatever medium it appears -- book, play, audio, or motion picture -- the story never fails to enthrall since the characters are so realistic you can rename them with people you know very well, and the plot with its culmination could not be more satisfying.

Why couldn't someone, then, update the story into a contemporary setting by redressing the characters and have the plot deal not merely with a terminally grouchy boss but, more importantly, with a dedicated atheist who loves to separate the public from its belief in God? – Well, someone has.

When I first met Steve Luhring and wanted to read this delightful adaptation, I asked him why he had written it. Without hesitation, he replied, "Because the story I most wanted to read hadn't been written yet, so I had to write it myself." I was astonished, since I gave virtually the same reply when people asked why I had written *A Skeleton in God's Closet*. For almost two thousand years, the plot in that book had been awaiting an author, so I finally felt compelled to write it myself. It became a #1 national best-seller in religious fiction, and I hope the same for *Scrooge and the Question of God's Existence*.

In these pages, we have not only some fun, fresh, and downright creative entertainment, but also a story with strong potential to do some good. As an author, I also write not merely to entertain, but to speak the truth, make the case, defend, persuade, and inspire -- qualities I saw in this adaptation as well. It would have been easier for me to wish the author luck and send him on his way, but instead I felt compelled to advise in the editing of the book and continue to promote it.

Scrooge and the Question of God's Existence is not simply an updated, though nearly identical, version of Dickens' great classic. That would border on plagiarism. Instead, Steve Luhring has made this retelling his own in some surprising and creative ways that I'll let you discover on your own, although here are some hints.

Luhring's tale deals with doubt, unbelief, pain, and the problem of evil. It's about making sense of the world we live in and coming to peace with matters of the head as well as the heart. While Charles Dickens' immortal story is a compelling tale of transformation, imagine what it would look like had Dickens been ambitious enough to have had Scrooge go on to tackle some of the greatest questions in life, such as: Does God exist? If so, why is there such evil and suffering in this world? Is there meaning and purpose in life? Is there an after-life? Is freedom worth fighting for, and what's at stake if we lose it? These pages are bold enough to do exactly that, and do it brilliantly.

They are also most certainly about atheists – both young and old, an increasing group in our secularizing society. C. S. Lewis once said "A young man who wishes to remain a sound atheist cannot be too careful of his reading." If any such are reading this book: Warning. Danger ahead! This story may evoke thoughts you had never pondered before!

In closing, I hope that once you've read this book, you may also discover that it's the story you most wanted to read.

-- Paul L. Maier

INTRODUCTION

"Jimmy, is that you, old friend?" the professor inquired breathlessly. There was a creak of a floorboard outside the study where Professor Edward Spassnicht stood, then another, then the rattle of the doorknob.

"Sir?" said the voice from just outside the study. Spassnicht's countenance shifted from anticipation to disappointment, realizing it was the housekeeper come to check on him and deliver his laundry. As she peaked her head through the doorway and entered he could tell by the look on her face that she was worried about him.

"You know, sir," she spoke in a gentle whisper, "that Jimmy has been dead for many years now?" Spassnicht nodded and managed a small grimace. When Spassnicht smiled this way it gave his otherwise wrinkly old face a boyish charm. After thanking her for checking in he dismissed her. As she left, he retreated to his desk. Sitting back in his leather chair with his feet resting on the desk of his home office, he stared out of his dimly lit office through the diamond-shaped panes of window into the night. Normally, the nighttime view from the third story of his spacious and comfortable, century-old townhouse was enviable.

Located in the affluent, historic Londontown neighborhood of Washington D.C., his residence was directly across the street from a small city park which was surrounded by generations-old Victorian style buildings. But tonight even nearby street lights were difficult to see because of the near blizzard conditions. The phone rang and he picked it up.

"Merry Christmas," the voice on the phone said.

"Merry Christmas to you too, Erin," he said smiling from ear to ear. With the sound of her voice the stress seemed to disappear from his face. "It's hard to believe that it was only five years ago that my old heart had failed me. I was balancing on a knife's edge between life and death and you, young lady, saved me."

"Yes, on the edge. I remember it well. Now what's this about your latest health troubles?" Erin Crandall asked. "I'm really worried."

With a calm detachedness, he explained, "The doctors told me today that they've discovered an aneurysm in an artery near my heart. It's like a time bomb waiting to explode and an explosion would mean a sudden … well, a sudden reason for my enemies to celebrate."

"You survived that prior mess, so you can tackle this as well." said Erin, attempting to say something hopeful. Spassnicht was like a father to her. There was a pause before she continued cautiously, "Since you survived your last brush with death, one could say 'you had lived to tell the tale,' but actually, you've chosen to keep the details of that night a secret. Won't you please reconsider now? Is the secret worth keeping at all?"

"Perhaps not, but I'm one step ahead of you." The small grimace returned to his face. He continued, "I've made plans to share my secret with the world. But let me just say I feel torn – it feels like a real dilemma. If I keep my story a secret, I betray my own conscience, which tells me the world needs to know. If I tell the story, I'm afraid …" Spassnicht's voice trailed off as the reflection of two headlights caught his eye. A car had just turned onto his street and in a moment had pulled up in front of his residence and stopped.

"Edward, are you still there? Is everything all right?"

"Of course – of course. I'm fine. I was just distracted. It seems my visitor has arrived." He paused. "I can't believe she actually ventured out in this weather."

"Perhaps we could continue this conversation later?" Erin inquired.

"Okay." murmured Spassnicht now quite distracted by the car outside. "Thank you. It was very kind of you to call. I'm fine and I will be fine. Say hello to your husband for me by the way."

Spassnicht ended the call and continued to peer intently out the window. A woman all wrapped in winter gear bounded out of the car and began a determined walk for his front door. The woman's scarf guarded her from the cold, but unfortunately, it guarded her identity from Spassnicht as well. Knowing the storm made waiting outside particularly unpleasant, he called to his housekeeper to greet his visitor as he slowly made his way to the first floor. He had turned seventy this year, and lately his knees were feeling their age on the stairs.

When Spassnicht and the woman met in the front hall, the woman spoke first. "Finally we meet face to face, Dr. Spassnicht. I'm Margaret Hatz. Thanks for agreeing to meet me. Do you recall that I interviewed you over the phone about five years ago about a new law you had lobbied to enact?"

Spassnicht nodded slowly. "Yes, I recall the interview. Welcome to my home."

"It was on the night after our interview that you seemed to have quite suddenly changed in your thinking on the hate speech law. That's why I called you. I'm looking for the inside scoop on the demise of that law. The biggest single factor in that law was *you* – first to get it passed, then to get it repealed. I want you to tell the world in your own words what happened that night that caused you to turn on a dime and change your views on ... well, on just about everything."

Spassnicht smiled politely. The invitation from the reporter to tell the world his untold story the same day that his life-threatening aneurysm had been discovered seemed almost providential. He knew that his time could be running out. Thanks to his aneurysm, he might not even have one more night on this earth. And against all odds, a reporter had called and was even willing to show up on short notice, in the middle of a blizzard no less. Perhaps it was a sign.

He had some reservations about sharing with the reporter, though. While he didn't know her well, she had been an ally *before* his transformation. Now that he had so publicly changed his views; philosophical, political, and theological; she might very well be an enemy. If she had the inside scoop, he couldn't be sure she'd do anything more than make a mockery of the parts of the story that were more difficult to believe and try to use them to discredit him. Yet the story needed to be shared. The events of that night had changed his life, after all. Perhaps the profound and edifying truths in the story would have a positive effect on this reporter and those she shared it with. And perhaps he simply needed to give her the benefit of the doubt for being a reasonably objective journalist. He decided to take his chances.

He smiled. "I'm ready to talk. Why don't we make our way into the living room? Can I get you something warm to drink? A cup of coffee, perhaps?"

"No thanks. I've been drinking it all day." she assured him and followed him from the hall into the living room, which ran along the front of the house.

"Please make yourself comfortable."

She sat down on the couch, then took out a recording device and placed it on the coffee table. "Please, Professor. Do you mind starting at the beginning?"

He stood behind a large wingback chair that stood adjacent to the couch, near the fireplace, grabbing it with both hands to steady himself as the thought of finally sharing his secret gave him an unexpected rush of nerves. "To start at the beginning means we start not with me, but with my colleague, James Merakis. To understand what happened to me the night of the transformation, one must first be clear about who Professor Merakis was."

"James Merakis? That's a name I haven't heard in years."

The details were burned into Spassnicht's memory like nothing else in his life. He'd resisted the urge to tell this story for several years, but once he started, the old rhetorical prowess took over. "During his life, James Merakis was bigger than life. He was a man that young men wanted to imitate, a cultural icon. I was not surprised when he became a bestselling author. He could communicate like few other men alive. He had a gift. When Jimmy spoke, people listened. Indeed, when he wrote, people read. He spoke using careful observation and a quick wit to draw people to hang on his every word. He had a bloodhound's sense for sniffing out the irony in any situation. Speaking to enormous crowds, he only took a moment to surprise them with his insights. He was always several steps ahead of the crowd in his thinking and his followers ran eagerly to catch up.

"But twelve years ago the headline read: 'Dr. James Merakis Succumbs to Long-Term Illness on Christmas Eve.' He was dead and therefore he had uttered his last words and written his last chapter for all eternity. At least that's what Jimmy would have told you. For on his view, a man lived and died ... and that was it. There was no hope for anything beyond this mortal life. If this is a dismal thought to some, it was something that Jimmy had found a way to overcome with the fulfillment that success brought him as well as the moral freedom his rejection of the afterlife allowed him. He excelled at rhetoric, but he excelled at fun too, which was another reason so many young men imitated him. He reasoned that if one doesn't exist after death, that precludes the possibility of getting punished after death. Suffice it to say Jimmy had rejected the idea of God as well. Not only had he rejected the idea of God, his rejection was his claim to fame. The idea of God was the very idea he sought to eradicate. He maintained that there was no such thing as a reasonable belief in the existence of God."

With that pronouncement, Spassnicht walked around the chair toward the window. There he came to a stop with his back to Ms. Hatz. He stared out the window at the winter storm that was only visible in the darkness by the faint glow of a few street lights. A strong gust of wind hit the building which initiated a chorus of creaks and groans. He rubbed his wrinkly chin once as if it might help bring the details in his memory into greater focus and continued to tell the story.

"There was a group of individuals that lived near the professor, followers of Christ, whom Jimmy found quaint, but annoying." Spassnicht grinned and continued. "They prayed for him to embrace God before his death. During the course of Jimmy's illness, those same Christians prayed for his healing and offered to help him in his time of need. They were a gung-ho bunch. He wrote off these overtures as a shameless publicity stunt and suggested that those praying had no sincere interest in their antagonist's well-being, only an interest in placing themselves on the moral high-ground and then shining a spotlight on themselves. In an attempt to pull the spotlight off them, he asked them not to pray, warned them not to invent false claims of a deathbed conversion, and told them to worry about themselves, not him."

"None of the Christians were permitted to his bedside, so none were in a position to make a claim of a deathbed conversion. Furthermore, there were no rogue nurses inventing stories of him calling out to God in his dying breath. So his fans took it as fact that he stayed consistent to the end – thumbing his nose at the idea of God."

He paused for a moment and turned toward the reporter. Looking her in the eyes and lowering his voice to a hush, he inquired, "But I ask you, what do we really know about the fact of the matter? Think of it: As a man stands utterly alone at the precipice of death -- with no light, no hope, no going back, and no one to call to for help or for even a simple answer -- does he make yet one last banal joke when there's no one to laugh? Can one ever be too sure of something as private as a man's dying thoughts?"

The winter wind outside rose again, creating a long, low, howl.

Ms. Hatz did not flinch, but instead gave Spassnicht a confused look. "Help me understand something. I know you were Merakis' colleague, but what do his life, death, and dying thoughts have to do with you?"

"You'll see in the end it has everything to do with me. I was more than just another person who mourned Jimmy's death. To call us two 'colleagues' seems inadequate. We shared the same *Weltanschauung*. I'm sorry – that means worldview. We worked together on the same cause, and were more like brothers than mere colleagues. On our view at the time, there was no afterlife, as I've mentioned, no soul, and no transcendent creator to assign transcending purpose to our existence. Instead we viewed life as 'matter-in-motion,' as 'complex dominos falling.' So to summarize, you lived, you died ... and that was it. And that was OK with us. In fact, we preferred it that way."

"Preferred it?" questioned the reporter.

"Yes, that's quite right. Now that poor Jimmy had passed, I felt it all the more necessary to do my part to stamp out belief in God and advance the 'more appealing' ideas of atheism and naturalism. Here I'm using the word, naturalism, to simply describe a view in which the foremost rule is 'no miracles allowed.'"

"Now, I have some serious issues with the church, as you may know, but can you help me understand why you had such a harsh reaction to religion?"

"Well, it was not what you're probably thinking -- a reaction to religiously motivated terrorism or because I was at odds with certain religious groups over social issues. There were other reasons, more private and more personal, which will be clear enough before too long. Regardless, this was an enormous calling, but one that I felt up to and found immensely satisfying. Since the passing of Jimmy, I was widely considered the world's most famous living atheist.

"My rise to fame over the last decade, concurrent with the rise of old Jimmy, had been a rewarding experience that bolstered my interest in this pursuit and served as confirmation that I was doing 'the right thing.' The harder I railed against organized religion and belief in God, the more attention I received, the more interviews I did, the more books I sold, the more money I made, and the more in general my star shone.

"So I had power and I used it against the religious, especially the dominant religious group -- the Christians. While followers of Christ were earnestly praying for the healing of my friend, Jimmy, I was preparing lawsuits against them for praying in public. Lawsuits were a favorite tool of mine. I was suing the religious without restraint for all their detrimental acts against society. Legislation was another favorite tool of mine, as you know. I was hoping someday to outlaw the public expression of religion all together. For on my view, publicly expressing a belief in God violated my right to freedom *from* religion."

He paused to see if the reporter had any additional questions at this point. When she had none, he proceeded to ask one of his own. "If you don't mind me asking, is my story of any personal significance to you? You interviewed me only hours before my transformation. Perhaps this would make the changes you see in me all the more real and all the more difficult to ignore."

"This is merely the subject of a story I'm writing for *The News*. That's where my interest ends. I appreciate your help – don't get me wrong, but I'm *not* on a personal quest for spiritual enlightenment, if that's what you're wondering."

Spassnicht's hopes of influencing her diminished and doubts about sharing his story began to resurface. He had only shared things that were public knowledge up to this point. It wasn't too late for him to stop before the hard-to-believe secrets were shared.

He decided to proceed with caution. "I should warn you -- it may be hard for you to believe some of the things I'm going to tell you. As far as believability goes, you should know that I myself find it all hard to believe, even though I experienced it firsthand. But early on I decided not to concern myself with whether it all was real and instead decided to focus on whether there was anything I might learn from the whole experience. Perhaps when we're done, you'll decide to take the same approach as I did."

"Hard to believe? In what way? Professor, please know in advance that, unlike much of your doting student fan club, I'm not inclined to simply believe whatever comes out of people's mouths. I find everything hard to believe." warned the reporter bluntly and with a laugh. "You call it a transformation. That's fine for you. I'm inclined to believe you just ... hmm, let's continue."

"I completely understand what you're saying," he assured her, masking his disappointment. But a light switch had gone off in his head. It became clear to him that he had made a mistake in agreeing to talk with the reporter. He feared that she had come only with hopes of getting the story and then using it to discredit him.

"Please, can we continue?" asked the reporter.

"You want the whole story, I assume?"

"I need to know the entire story, the whole truth," she demanded, still smiling but also looking impatient.

He sat down, leaned back to get very comfortable, grabbed his cup of tea, took a long sip, and began as if retelling an epic tale. "Well, to begin with, it all started in the land of unicorns."

The reported blinked in confusion.

"I'm sorry. I just made that up," he said as the childish smile on his wrinkly old face returned.

"Well, do you intend to tell me the real story or not?"

He paused, as if to prepare the reporter for his decision, then continued, "I really don't know if you're ready for the truth about that night. I'm sorry to have wasted this much of your time, but I just don't think I can help you."

"Tell me you're not serious. You are going to tell me the story, right?"

As soon as the word, no, came from his lips, she interjected, "I can't believe I bothered to come here!" The reporter switched off the recorder and gathered her things to leave. "I suspected all along that you merely got a little flaky in your senior years. Now I'm positive. This is a lot of trouble over nothing," she scoffed as she made a hasty move for the front door. "Unicorns? You haven't stopped talking to the media in the last several years about all your new philosophical, political, and religious views – but when asked for the story behind your improbable change, you bring up unicorns! What kind of daffy nonsense." and with the last comment she gave a cross look at the professor and then ducked her head as she bounded out into the storm.

"I'm sorry. That unicorn bit sounded much funnier in my head than you're finding it now I can see." he offered politely, still smiling as he stood in the open doorway, "Um, drive safe." A moment later, he watched her drive away. With the reporter gone, the cold reality of his dilemma returned and he began to ponder again what to do. He realized now that he had nearly walked into a disaster. Regardless of whether he told his story to a friend or an enemy, his enemies would eventually get the story and use the more unbelievable parts to mock him and discredit him. He had to protect himself – yet the story had to be told.

He slowly made his way back up to his office, anxiously thinking about what he should do. Once in his office, he began pacing around the room, unable to sit still. There was no sound except for the howl of the storm outside and the creak of the hardwood floors as he walked. The grim thought of possibly dying crept back into his mind, but to force it out he redoubled his pacing and refocused back on a matter he had more control over -- sharing his story. He was distracted again when his eye was drawn to a dark corner of his office. High up on his massive bookcase, a book was conspicuously sticking out from the rest in its row. It was an area of the bookcase he hadn't touched in years. It struck him as odd that one book should be out of place. He rebuked himself for his lack of focus, but he knew he would continue to be distracted until the book was back in line. As he walked over to push it back into alignment with the others, the wind outside howled harder than ever, and the building creaked and groaned like it was alive.

When he was close enough, he could see it was a beautiful old hardcover book that he'd forgotten he had. It was just out of reach, though. He'd need the stepstool. Once he'd retrieved the stool and taken the two steps up, he could easily make out the title of the book – and when he'd read it, the answer to his conundrum became clear. A smile came to his face as he pulled the book off the shelf and began examining it with a joy that comes when a great riddle is finally solved. He would tell the story of that night five years ago – or more precisely, he would write the story. He would not write it as an autobiography, however; he would write it as fiction… as an adaptation, in fact.

For the book in his hand was *A Christmas Carol* by Charles Dickens. While the world is full of irritable old men just as it had been in the days of Dickens, the alias of Scrooge was particularly suitable in Spassnicht's case, given not only the past temperament of the man, but his story as well. Not only could he play the part of Ebenezer Scrooge, Jimmy Merakis could play the part of Scrooge's partner, Jacob Marley. With the story written as fiction, Spassnicht would pre-empt any debate about whether the events were real and whether he was crazy or not. The important truths he had learned that night would still be there, even if the events themselves were presented as fiction.

Although it was getting late, he sat down at his computer to begin at once. He began to type, "To begin with, Marley was dead. This must be distinctly understood or nothing wonderful can come of the story I am going to relate."[1]

Of course when he said Marley, he meant old Jimmy Merakis. Spassnicht admired his first few sentences with a smile. His expression then turned serious for a moment as he wondered, "Should this be in the present day or in Dickens' day? … I'd hate to lose the magic of Dickens' age, but my particular story is a modern one. So, present day it will be."

He then typed up the background just as he had shared it with the reporter. Upon completing the background, he paused for a moment to think about how to continue. "Oh yes," the aged professor said merrily in his empty office to no one in particular, "I know where to go next." And he began to type again, "While you may have already answered for yourself the question, 'Does God exist?,' there will be much to consider in what is forthcoming so I promise you'll soon have better grounds for answering this question and making a judgment. For now, I ask that you set aside any pre-judgments and resist the urge to go stampeding to conclusions. Better instead to start on the night of Scrooge's transformation, five years ago, on Christmas Eve ..."

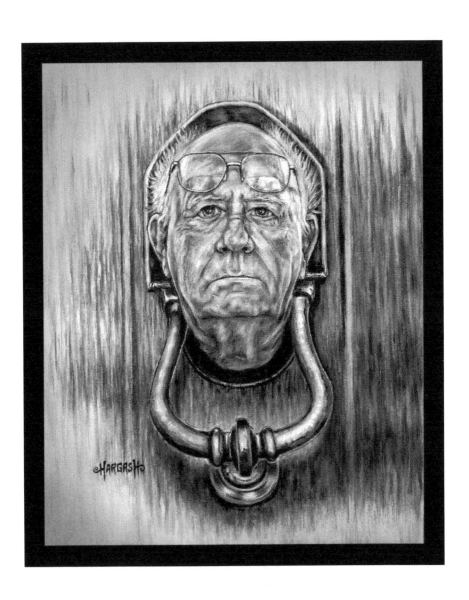

STAVE I – MARLEY'S GHOST

It was Christmas Eve and Emily Cratchit, mother of three, was in a flurry of Christmas-related preparations in the Cratchit home. Christmas Eve always came too soon for the Cratchit household and this year in particular she was at her wits end. Her work came to a halt when she heard her daughter, Martha, call out in protest. "Mom! Did you hear how Peter's talking to me?"

Emily took a breath and marched from her bedroom into the family room, reluctantly ready to play the role of referee between two of her children. Although ignoring them crossed her mind, it was not a great option. Since the quarters were tight, a shouting match between the two children that might follow would be difficult to ignore. "OK. What's the matter now?" she inquired.

After detailing far more background than was necessary to answer her mother's question, Martha concluded, "Then I said that someday I planned to have a much larger Christmas tree in my home than the wimpy one we currently have ... someday when I am married," Martha explained.

Emily's older son, Peter, jumped in. "And all I said was, 'Who'd marry you?'"

"I'll get married someday as long as he doesn't find out I'm related to you!"

"Are either of you using kind words?" Emily interjected, realizing that the two were arguing over nonsense, again. She'd expected this from her kids when they were younger, perhaps, but always imagined they'd know better by this age. Peter was 17 years old, and Martha was 11.

Martha continued her protest, "Do you know what he told Tiny Tim yesterday? He told him that he wasn't really part of our family – that he was a trained monkey that you and Dad adopted. He also told Tim that if he misbehaved he was going to sell him to the circus!" Then turning to Peter she declared, "That isn't funny."

"Peter, how could you?"

Peter rolled his eyes. "I was just joking with him—*obviously*."

"He's only four. Did he know you were joking?"

Martha jumped in again. "Peter thinks he's so funny, but Tim asked me, 'Martha, I'm a real person, right?' See? He wasn't sure. He'll believe anything Peter tells him. He's too little to know better."

"Peter, I know you love your brother, but it mystifies me why you insist on amusing yourself at his expense. Please stop terrorizing your brother," Emily instructed.

"You're right about one thing – I do love little T and he knows it. I think that he'd actually be OK with being a monkey. I wouldn't tease him if I didn't think he was secure enough to take it. And if Martha wasn't so … like herself, she could take a joke too."

"Tim is not OK with being a monkey. That's ridiculous." Martha objected.

"I don't have time to referee you two right now. We all have a lot to do before your father gets home from church and it will go better for everyone if we do it with a little kindness." Emily hoped that would be the end of it and was grateful that these nonsensical arguments were about the only trouble her children managed to cause. The Cratchit home was typically a peaceful place, but for the last several weeks, the tension had been unusually high, especially between Emily and her teenage son. In addition to Emily's stress, something had been eating Peter, but Emily had no idea what it was. Peter had a gift for making light of things, but lately everyone and everything had become fair game – almost nothing was sacred.

Peter's cell phone began to ring and he took this as his cue to escape from the scene, retreating to his bedroom. Emily also took this as a welcome end of the discussion and made her way back to her bedroom to continue her work, but as she passed Peter's door, she overheard Peter's voice as he talked to his friend on the phone.

"I really don't want to go to church tomorrow. You don't know how lucky you are that your parents don't go to church." There was a pause as Peter listened. "No, there's *no* way I can get out of it. My dad's, um, the pastor. ... Right, Scrooge is cool. Scrooge says Christmas is wishful thinking by the weak-minded and closed-minded masses. He's a pretty smart guy. ... I can't take that stuff that's going on in church too seriously, either. ... I don't really get into reading, but sure, I'll check it out. Thanks, bro. Scrooge will be celebrating reason this season. Maybe I'll join him."

With that, Peter ended the call. Emily was in shock. She had no idea her son was thinking this way. Did she just hear her son say that he would be celebrating reason this season with Scrooge? *Peter will not be happy that I eavesdropped on his conversation*, she thought, *but this is too serious to ignore*. She tapped on the door and stuck her head into his room.

There was an awkward silence in the room as Emily struggled with how to begin. The words of her son's phone conversation had hurt her deeply. Her first instinct was to burst into a ten minute diatribe directed at her son, which she knew would not be effective. Unfortunately, the stress of the holidays or the lack of sleep got the best of her, and she felt a rush of negative emotions as she struggled to think of what to say. Finally, she simply asked, "Why?"

"Mom, please!" Peter said in disgust. "Were you eavesdropping?"

Crying was not characteristic for Emily, but against her own will her eyes began to tear up in frustration. She was normally strong and determined. Furthermore, she knew her son's criticism of "weak-minded" did not apply to her by a long shot. She was well educated, having studied at a top biomedical studies program on the east coast. She had had a promising career in the medical sciences field, during which she'd been promoted to director of a hematology laboratory at Providence hospital right in Londontown, but she had put that career on hold in order to raise her family and support her husband's ministry as head pastor of a large church. Even so, Emily suspected that her son, like many adolescents, had in his mind made a downward adjustment to the perceived IQs of his parents by one standard deviation or so.

Extremely embarrassed that she was in tears, she quickly regained her composure and attempted so show Peter some strength. "The church has valid reasons for all of the doctrines it holds. I heard you accuse the church of being closed-minded ... but don't you be so open-minded that your brain falls out.[2] Don't trade your discernment and reason in for an extra helping of open-mindedness. When people like Scrooge give you their views, don't just agree with them because they're the latest to go rattling through your head."

"Mom, is it possible he's right and you're wrong? Maybe Christmas is just a fairytale for people afraid of the dark?"

"It's also possible that Scrooge's atheism is nothing more than a fairytale for people afraid of the light.[3]" Emily replied in a somewhat defensive tone. In truth, she did not want to talk about this. She simply wanted her son to believe, like her. It made her sad to think that her son was doubting his faith. But even if she had wanted to continue the conversation, she wouldn't be getting the chance. Peter walked right past her on his way out of the room, grabbed his winter coat and hat off the family room couch, and walked out the front door of the apartment with a cool nonchalance. As she watched him go, a feeling of failure washed over her. She was glancing around the room, a bit lost as to what she should do next, when her eye caught an old picture of Peter hanging on the bedroom wall. In the picture, Peter was much younger and sporting a chubby-cheeked smile. Those happy, uncomplicated days seemed a like a lifetime ago. Again, her eyes welled with tears.

***

Meanwhile, across town a man was meeting with a team of lawyers in their office near a university campus where he was a distinguished professor. But rather than discussing whom to sue next, they were discussing an important bit of current events – new legislation that had been passed – and what it meant to their tireless cause. The man's name was Scrooge. His cause was to create a society free from religion.

The lawyers' conference room was full as they all sat around a large oak table. Scrooge, always so relaxed that it made all of his lawyers around him nervous, sat back with his feet up on the table as if he were relaxing in his family room. On the speaker phone was reporter Marissa Hessen, seeking comments from Scrooge for an article she was writing regarding the implications of this recently passed bill.

"You must be very pleased about the passage of this legislation, Professor Scrooge," Ms. Hessen began. "I understand you were a big player behind the scenes lobbying to get it passed. Because of your efforts we seem to have reached a watershed moment in the fight against hate crimes."

"Thank you. You're too kind," replied Scrooge.

"The timing of the bill's passage is remarkable, really. Within a week of the bill's passage, we witnessed a tragic hate crime, the assault of a member of the Love Without Limits community. The LWLs are of course known for their liberated lifestyle choices. The investigation has uncovered that the man charged with the assault attended services at First Evangelical Church here in Londontown. The authorities have it in a written confession that he listened to a sermon there – a sermon loaded with LWL-phobic, bigoted, hate speech. Based on your understanding, what will be the likely sentence for an individual found guilty under this new hate speech law?"

One of the lawyers on Scrooge's team chimed in, "If found guilty, the person who is the source of the hate speech can be charged with violating this law. This will be a test case, so it is difficult to guess about sentencing, but the law is written such that there will likely be significant jail time for the person who is the source of the hate speech."

Ms. Hessen interrupted, "If you could lean into the mic a bit, that might help, but I might have missed something. Can you help me understand how a person's speech makes him or her responsible for the actions of another?"

"Sorry." The lawyer continued, "The assault and the hate speech are two separate crimes involving two separate people, but the reason we happen to know about the latter is because of the police's investigation of the former. So if someone speaks out against the LWL, that is enough. No additional crime need take place."

"Thanks for clarifying. I follow. Do you know the pastor's name?"

"We certainly do." answered the lawyer eagerly. "Reverend Bob Cratchit. As I understand it from the media, they expect the authorities to produce a warrant for the arrest of this prominent pastor any day now."

Ms. Hessen replied. "Sounds like he'd be a good person to talk to as well. This legislation really raises the stakes for those churches that want to publicly hold to an anti-LWL point of view."

"Oh yes! Penalties for violating the law include fines and jail-time for any individuals involved, not to mention large fines and loss of tax-exempt status for any non-profit found sponsoring the hate speech. Pastor Bob and First Evangelical Church are in the crosshairs of the law. It should be a complete knock-out. There's plenty of evidence in this case."

"Also, if you step back and look at the inevitable big picture impact, every conservative religious denomination in the country who speaks against the LWL's "Love Without Limits" platform will find themselves on the wrong side of the law. They won't know what hit them!" Scrooge said with a laugh.

"How long have you been an advocate for LWL rights?"

Scrooge paused for a moment as if to prepare his interviewer for his response. "Oh, I'm not an LWL rights advocate in any meaningful sense. I'm an atheist, and my efforts are aimed at creating a society free from religion. That's where my motivation lies, and I've made no secrets about it. I'm just taking my friends where I can find them. And I assume the advocates of non-traditional lifestyles can do the same."

After a long pause, the voice on the phone replied, "Well, thank you for your time and help. Oh, and I look forward to seeing you on TV soon in the Celebrity Civil Rights Celebration in a couple days. I hope we can talk again in the near future. This has been very valuable to me."

After the phone call ended, Scrooge thanked his team of lawyers and dismissed them. As the first lawyer opened the door to leave, Scrooge's nephew, Fred, pushed his way in and cried cheerfully, "A merry Christmas, uncle!"

The entrance of Fred; a barrel-chested man in his late twenties with a friendly face, an effortless grin, and a booming voice; grabbed the attention of all in the room. While Fred's gregarious presence dominated nearly any room he entered, his spirit could not have been more out of place in this instance. His words were met with silence and blank stares from Scrooge's lawyers as if he were speaking a foreign language. Scrooge, on the other hand, simply rolled his eyes upon recognizing his nephew.

Fred, earnestly trying to get a response from his uncle, repeated his greeting. "A merry Christmas, uncle!"

Scrooge replied, "Christmas? Bah! Humbug!"[4]

As the last of the lawyers filed out of the room, he walked by Fred and within a couple inches of Fred's face looked up and mumbled in derision, "You know it's a myth."

"Very pleasant, aren't you?" replied Fred grimacing down at the lawyer as he pushed his way out of the room, not looking back at Fred. Redirecting his attention toward his uncle, Fred continued, "That's really a wonderful trick – I didn't even see your lips move as you pulled his string." When Scrooge did not respond, he continued, "Christmas a humbug, uncle! You don't mean that, I'm sure?"

"I do," said Scrooge. "Merry Christmas! What right have you to be merry? What *reason* have you to be merry? The Christmas story is a myth, in case you missed the point a moment ago. You believe in a myth! If I could work my will, every idiot who goes about with 'Merry Christmas' on his lips, should be boiled with his own pudding, and buried with a stake of holly through his heart."

"Uncle!"

"Nephew! Keep Christmas in your own way, and let me keep it in mine."

"Keep it! But you don't keep it."

"Let me leave it alone, then. Much good may it do you! Much good it has ever done you!"[5]

"Christmas has done me good, the ultimate good I'd say. I believe its promises and it gives me hope for beyond the grave. Life is utterly absurd and meaningless without a loving God. I have nothing to lose and eternity to gain. And I feel great joy in serving my Creator."

"Karl Marx liked to call what you feel the opium of the masses. Can I just tell you that you sound like a fool?" Scrooge stood energetically as he made his point, then turned his back to Fred and walked over to the corner of the room to retrieve his winter coat.

"Uncle, I believe the Christmas story is true, I really do. I have every good reason to believe it and have no convincing reason to doubt it. Let's reason about it together." Fred offered with a grin.

"If Christmas and all of Christianity is not a myth, then why is God so hidden?" questioned Scrooge in a dismissive tone.

Fred had clearly been hoping Scrooge would engage him with questions and jumped at the challenge, but tried to hide the excitement he felt having finally gotten Scrooge to open the door to this line of discussion. So he calmly took a seat, leaned forward with his hands on his knees and continued, "Perhaps the very nature of God makes it such that we as finite creatures cannot look directly upon him. But as with the sun, while we can't look directly at it, we can't see our world without it."[6]

"I can see the world without God quite nicely, thank you."

"You say that, but why is the world even here, and what's it all for? Can you explain why it exists? Why is there something, rather than nothing after all?"[7]

Scrooge paused and pretended to think carefully, pulled his coat on, and then said with a sneer, "I don't care. Now you need to listen to me. You may have gotten an A+ in Sunday school for faithfully repeating what your teachers said, but I've given the best years of my life to scholarly work ..."

"Now wait. Why is there something rather than nothing, Uncle? It's a profound question that a thoughtful person would consider before dismissing the idea of God. In fact, many have started with that question only to have their thoughts lead them all the way to God."

"It's profound to you perhaps, but it's a hum-bug to me."

Fred continued, "In faith there is enough light for those who want to believe and enough shadows to blind those who don't.[8] You say God is hidden, but you close your eyes to the explanation for the universe that has been written on man's heart since the beginning. God, as an explanation for the universe, is something that rings true to me. God's creation is evidence of God himself. I believe the reason there is something rather than nothing is because, dear uncle, God created it! You ask why God is hidden. Maybe the simple answer is that he wants us to make a choice of the heart to seek him that we simply could not make if he first overpowered mankind with a tautology of his existence. Admit it, uncle – it is possible that God exists."

Scrooge repeated rotely: "It's possible that God exists." Then he continued sharply, "It's just *terribly* unlikely in my view – so unlikely that it's not worth considering. I know this will hurt your feelings, but I can't respect a person such as yourself who believes in miracles. Quite honestly, they strike me as ridiculous. Miracles are quite amusing. And oh! What fun! Yes, like when an old lady sees the face of a saint in a potato chip and every fool proclaims – it's a miracle!"

Fred replied in a firm but pleasant manner, "So if one miracle claim turns out to be false or even patently ridiculous, then all the rest are guilty of being false? Guilt by association, right? It makes sense to me that if God exists and created the universe, then any other miracle you imagine is too difficult for God is in fact a piece of cake compared to the creation of the universe out of nothing. If you don't have certainty on the origin of the universe and the existence of God, why do you think you can rule out miracles right off the bat?"

Scrooge had completed the gathering up of his things to leave. In an attempt to end the conversation, he replied hurriedly, "OK then, I've changed my mind. I do believe in one miracle – it's a miracle that I'm still entertaining this ridiculous conversation. Good afternoon! I'm sure you have other important things to do as well. Perhaps, my miracle-loving nephew, you're singing Christmas carols later with the Tooth Fairy?"

Fred didn't waste his time taking offense at his uncle's teasing and instead stayed true to his original purpose. "Uncle, I do have plans for later, but I was hoping to include you. That's actually why I'm here – to invite you over for Christmas dinner tomorrow."

"You can't be serious!" Scrooge scoffed as he walked out of the office and onto the street with Fred following close behind.

"Yes, I am! Come! Dine with us tomorrow."[9]

"I'd dine in Hades first! Good afternoon."

"I want nothing from you; I ask nothing of you; why can't we be friends?"

"Good afternoon," said Scrooge more firmly.

"I am sorry, with all my heart, to find you so resolute. But I have made my visit in the spirit of Christmas, and I'll keep my Christmas humor to the last. So a Merry Christmas, uncle!"

"Good afternoon!" said Scrooge[10] as he stormed down the street in the direction of his office on campus, leaving Fred behind.

It was near the end of the day, and it was cold and getting colder. The setting sun was entirely hidden by fog that was billowing in, providing a gloomy, dream-like ambience for his walk. The diffused, dim daylight that remained was vanishing quickly. House lights and streetlights were now casting a hazy glow into the street. As he walked, he replayed the conversation with his nephew in his head. *Fred's probably pretty proud of himself for that little performance. What a fool. I'm not so cruel as to do it, but all I had to do is ask him about my little sister, his mother. One of the gentlest, sweetest creatures on the planet – dead and gone. Where was God when she died on the delivery table giving birth to Fred?* Upon reaching his office, he hurriedly closed up for the day.

His own health was the furthest thing from his mind. A million other thoughts occupied him—his triumphs, his plans, his idiotic nephew. But suddenly he became aware of a terrible, unsettling feeling within him and felt the need to grab his chest. He struggled for breath and felt as though he was suffocating. A feeling of doom that he could not shake flooded over him. His mind raced to figure out what was wrong. His heart pounded unusually fast and with unmistakable irregularity. Feeling faint, he sat down in his desk chair, gasping for air. His chest was now tight, painfully tight, and a deep, satisfying breath was impossible to get. Fear washed over him like an unexpected wave. After a minute of trying, a minute that seemed like a lifetime, he did catch his breath and regained a bit of confidence.

Since most at the university had left for home early that day in preparation for imminent Christmas celebrations, the building was quiet … perhaps too quiet. A little noise would have been welcomed by Scrooge – to make him feel as though things were normal after having just endured this very unsettling experience. He now felt reasonably normal again and rose to leave the office for home.

He slowly gathered his things and moved toward the door to leave, but before he reached the door he heard a sudden quick whisper, spoken just as one does when conveying a secret meant to be heard by only one person: "It's your time."

The unexpected voice chilled him to the bone. His mind raced. Had he imagined it? Perhaps someone had spied his little episode and was having a little fun with him. Perhaps it was a trick of some sort. He did a careful walk around the small office to search for clues to this mystery, but found none. If someone was in fact playing a trick on him by talking in a scary voice from a hiding place, Scrooge could find no clues of their existence. Perhaps it was a voice from another room and he had merely overheard a bit of some other conversation. He stood silently to see if he could hear anything else, but there was not a peep. The office was dead silent. Everyone in the building had no doubt gone home for the day and he was alone. The experience of hearing the voice was very strange and very unwelcome. Worst of all, there was a lack of evidence to settle the matter.

"Perhaps I'm simply losing my mind," he thought, trying to dismiss the occurrence.

Now the average man may use this rationalization, "I'm losing my mind," at a drop of a hat, but for Scrooge this was really a remarkable admission. To entertain, if only in his private thoughts, that he was possibly losing his mind was an almost unprecedented show of humility. He viewed his mental faculties as virtually inerrant. His mighty intellect was inseparable from his sense of self-worth, so this admission was not without a great, albeit secret, cost. In Scrooge's rationalization, though, losing one's mind was a more likely explanation than anything of a supernatural variety.

"What does 'It's your time' really mean? A bit ambiguous, I think." He then added, "Bah! Humbug!"[11] in a most irritated and defiant manner as he left his office and headed for home.

As he walked down the sidewalk in the early dark of winter, the fog surrounded him. The distance from Scrooge's office to home was relatively short, taking him from the edge of campus where his office was, across the main street of Londontown, and then through a half dozen or so city blocks of mostly residential housing to his townhouse bordering a city park. About midway through Scrooge's walk home, an unusually slow and careful walk, there was a large church with a small cemetery amidst the houses that Scrooge used as a milestone to mark the halfway point in his walk home. Since the time when Scrooge was young he'd always been uncomfortable in cemeteries. As a boy he had made a habit of holding his breath whenever he went by one, but since soon he began to view that as a ridiculous habit, he replaced it with the habit of whistling. *Cemeteries! -- what an awful reminder of the end of it all*, Scrooge thought to himself as he began to whistle. He picked a happy tune – something to cheer himself up and block any unpleasant realities from his mind, but he still felt very weak and his whistling suffered. *Even "Zip-A-Dee Doo-Dah" sounds like a requiem*, he thought to himself in frustration.

When Scrooge was several steps past the graveyard and still not done whistling, a young man approached Scrooge from the opposite direction quite suddenly through the shadows and thick fog. "Mr. Scrooge, is that you?" cracked the voice of the young man loudly as he approached. "Can I just tell you you're awesome? You and Mr. Marley are the reason I'm leaving the church. Religious people are such idiots, you know?"

To Scrooge, the approach of the young man was sudden and unwelcome. Scrooge was normally quite deft in handling fans, but at the moment he was feeling quite awful. He was also very unimpressed with this boy's appearance and the way he spoke. "What specifically in my writing made the difference to you?" Scrooge asked in a skeptical, impatient tone, unable to hide his displeasure.

"I don't know – all of it? I just love the way you show religious freaks for the freaks that they are!" said the young man, perhaps trying to impress Scrooge with his conviction.

Scrooge was not impressed. Quite the opposite. His weakened condition left him without an ounce of patience and so he responded to this boy in a manner he usually reserved for his opponents – that is to say, he let the boy have it. "First of all, my colleague's name is Dr. Marley, Dr. Jacob Marley, not Mr. Marley. And I'm Dr. Scrooge, not Mr. Scrooge in case you're wondering. If you were so familiar with Dr. Marley's and my writings, I'd think you'd know our names, including titles. But perhaps you don't know that it's courtesy to call people by their proper titles, so let me be the first to tell you. I'm a doctor. I've earned a doctorate. I've earned that title. Show respect! Second of all, I'm not interested in a fan club of teenagers who believe something because it's popular or because I'm popular." He then drew an uneasy breath and continued, "I don't have time for this conversation right now. I must be going. My parting advice for you is to *think for yourself*. I find it repulsive and weak when people borrow the intellectual capital of others. Yes, religious people are idiots. Why? Oh, because so-and-so says so. It's a pitiful appeal to authority and intellectually lazy!" As he said all this, his chest began to ache terribly, and as he rubbed at it, he wondered if he should consider taking an aspirin or something.

The young fan, seeing him in distress, looked worried. "Are … are you okay, Dr. Scrooge? Can I help you?"

Scrooge, now regretting the tirade, asked, "I'm embarrassed to have to ask, but do you by a wild chance have any aspirin? It's … for a headache – a headache you've just brought on." Of course the aspirin were not for a headache, but Scrooge felt it was a convenient lie that allowed him to save face.

Now, nine people out of ten would have either punched Scrooge in the nose, run off crying, or stamped off in a huff after receiving a lecture such as the one Scrooge had just delivered, but the young fan, although a bit surprised by Scrooge's tirade, was seemingly unhurt by Scrooge's comments and still eager to help. "Uh, yeah, actually, I do have aspirin. I've got you covered." The young man pulled a pill bottle out of his jacket pocket, opened it, and shook a couple of small white tablets into Scrooge's hand. "My friends won't believe me when I tell them I met you."

"Then give them this." said Scrooge as he handed the boy a business card with his signature on the back. Scrooge was proud of himself for thinking of something gracious to do like sharing a business card with the fanboy in spite of the inopportune circumstances. Scrooge took the aspirin right there on the sidewalk with water from his water bottle that he carried in his briefcase. He popped the aspirin in his mouth, tilted back his head, and took several careful gulps of water until he was sure the aspirin were down where they could do some good. When Scrooge had finished he noticed that the young man had already disappeared into the fog without a goodbye or even a sound.

Still feeling a bit shaken, he continued his slow and careful walk. Upon reaching his townhouse, he climbed the stairs to his front door. Normally a staircase he could take without a second thought, this short climb left him feeling sick and light headed. He felt short of breath again. Scrooge was at war with himself. In one moment he reproached himself for the fearful feeling he had, and in the next moment he was in near panic again, struggling for control of the symptoms that were so inescapable. After a moment of internal conflict, which Scrooge imagined to a person observing from the street would simply look like a strange, old man staring blankly at his front door, Scrooge felt a moment of relief and resolved to press on. Then, upon having his key in the lock of the door, he saw in the door knocker, without its undergoing any intermediate process of change—not a knocker, but Marley's face.[12]

Marley's face. It was not angry or ferocious, but looked at Scrooge as Marley used to look: with ghostly spectacles turned up on its ghostly forehead. The hair was curiously stirred, as if by breath or hot air. The eyes were wide open, though they were perfectly motionless. The eyes and the livid color of the face made it horrible to behold, but its horror seemed to be in spite of its facial expression and beyond its control.[13]

A moment later, before Scrooge's transfixed gaze, the knocker became simply a knocker again. Scrooge was too nervous and bewildered to do anything but continue to stare at the knocker. His thoughts raced. Had he imagined it? Was he losing his mind? Didn't he have enough to worry about with his sudden ill-health? He had no time for this distraction. He was tired and late for a date with his pillow. With this conviction, Scrooge proceeded through the doorway.

He did pause, with a moment's irresolution, before he shut the door to look cautiously behind it first, as if he half expected to be terrified with the sight of Marley's posterior sticking out into the hall. But there was nothing on the back of the door, except the screws and nuts that held the knocker on, so he said "Bah. Humbug!" and closed it with a bang.[14]

He then added with a snicker, "That would be a miracle." But despite this attempt at dismissing the apparition, the event was very strange and not so easy to dismiss. Scrooge stood in his large, two-story foyer. The only source of light came from a small antique lamp on a small table near the front door. It cast long shadows up the familiar wide staircase and across the walls. The staircase led to the second floor walkway that encircled the foyer on three sides and was bordered with a tall banister. The walkway was bordered by several doors and an enclosed staircase which led to the third floor where Scrooge's bedroom was located. Scrooge stood and contemplated what had happened and then thought of the pills the boy had given him. *What was in those pills?* thought Scrooge, *I was a bit rude to him. What if he slipped me some kind of hallucinogenic drug? What's more likely these days – that a kid is carrying aspirin or that he's carrying some hallucinogens? I shudder to think.*

Even more slowly and carefully, Scrooge proceeded up the stairs, noticing every beat of his heart, which was unusually fast and hard. By now, it seemed like a lifetime ago that he'd last felt normal, and he wondered if he'd ever feel normal again. He thought of the graveyard, and then a morbid thought of a more personal kind crept into his head – he wondered if he'd face Marley's fate tonight, the very anniversary of Marley's death. Then before panic could grip him even harder, he forced himself to put the thought out of his mind. He reached the landing at the top of the stairs on the third floor and entered his bedroom. It was a fairly lavish space for a house this old, with its own fireplace and a four-poster bed. The gas fireplace had no doubt been turned on by the housekeeper in anticipation of his arrival home. It was her custom to do so, anyway. It was currently burning low and the dim light gave the room a creepy air. Perhaps still rattled from the voice at the office, not to mention the experience at his front door, Scrooge decided to make sure his room was secure. Nobody under the bed; nobody in the closet; nobody in his bathrobe, which was hanging up in a suspicious attitude against the wall. Quite satisfied, he closed his door and locked himself in, which was not his usual custom.[15]

What a night! What could he do now but go to bed and get a good night's rest? He took comfort that both his housekeeper and butler were with him, somewhere within his huge, three story domicile. If he needed help, he had only to page them over the intercom on his bedside phone.

But was locking the door wise? He didn't want to lock out any help should he need it. He unlocked the door and decided that if he experienced any more trouble, he'd call the butler to take him to the emergency room at once, though the ER was the last place he wanted to be on Christmas Eve. It would be a zoo there. ERs were notoriously busy on holidays. Therefore, he made a plan to lie down and get some rest, which would no doubt improve his situation.

Scrooge would not make it to his bed tonight, though, for as soon as he had the thought, he was struck with a terrible, stabbing pain in the back. He lost his breath again but could not catch it this time. He was paralyzed by the pain. He dropped to his hands and knees; then a blurred moment later, he lost consciousness and collapsed to the floor completely. Scrooge was perfectly powerless, perfectly quiet, and perfectly still.

***

When Scrooge came to, he was in a different state of mind all together – more perceptive of the world around him. He could hear clearly, see clearly, and think more clearly than he could remember. And unlike his sorry state a few moments before, where with every slow step on the stairs his mind focused fearfully on his every bodily symptom, he now found his mind focused – outward, without an adverse bodily symptom to distract his remarkable concentration. What a joy this change of events brought him!

"Has ever a man recovered so quickly from such a horrid previous state?" Scrooge wondered aloud.

Then much to his surprise he heard his words repeated slowly in a powerful, deep voice that seemed to mock him. "Has ever a man recovered so quickly from such a horrid previous state?"

The voice startled him and would have startled anyone. He knew the voice. It was that of his old colleague and friend, Jacob Marley. There was no sight of the seven-years-dead man himself, though, only his voice. An instant later, in dramatic fashion, Marley passed right through the heavy door with a hearty laugh and without so much as the door opening a crack or even the rattle of a door knob. Upon his coming in, the dying flame in the hearth leapt up, as though it cried, "I know him; Marley!" and fell again.[16]

The sudden intrusion robbed Scrooge of the initial peace of the earlier moment. "What is the meaning of this?" he demanded in a voice meant to show impunity, but revealing a good deal of uncertainty and fear instead.

Slowly and forcefully Marley commanded, "Step back."

Scrooge obliged if for no other reason than to get a safer distance away from his visitor, but was shocked at what appeared on the floor before him. It was his own body – flesh and blood. And what was he now? Whatever he was, he had not stepped backwards *over* the body, but *through* it.

"What is the meaning of all this?" Scrooge asked again in a frenzied voice this time.

"It's your time," Marley replied, using the same words Scrooge heard in his head earlier in his office. "Are you ready?"

Scrooge did not reply, but stared blankly at Marley in bewilderment.

"You don't believe in me," observed Marley.

"I don't," said Scrooge.

"What evidence would you have of this reality beyond that of your senses?"

"I don't know."

"Why do you doubt your senses?"

"Because a little thing affects them. A slight disorder of the stomach makes them falter. You may be an undigested bit of beef, a blot of mustard, a crumb of cheese, a fragment of an underdone potato. There's more of gravy than of grave about you, whatever you are. Humbug, I tell you! Humbug!"[17]

"Look down and see yourself. Your time is short!"

"I've had a very bad night." conceded Scrooge euphemistically, suddenly feeling quite sorry for himself.

"You're nearly dead! But keep in mind, this is not the worst thing that could happen to you. For it is said that God uses our happiness to draw us to him, but only like a child is drawn to the light of a firefly, but God uses our trouble to draw us to Him in another way, transforming that light of a firefly into the light of a lighthouse in a storm. But you, Scrooge, up to this point have been like a grizzled, old seaman with his back to the light, quite enamored by the dark."

"Why do you, Marley of all people, speak of God as if he were real?"

"Your time is short. See me, if you are not fully blind. And hear now what I say. You've swallowed some big lies in your lifetime. They taste so wonderful to you that you've overlooked their danger. But rest assured the lies you swallowed are like cheese in a mouse trap. And when the mouse takes the cheese ..." Marley stopped to let Scrooge finish the analogy in his head and then continued, "The trigger on the mousetrap has been sprung. The hammer races toward your neck!"

Scrooge pleaded, "I want to live. I want to be well again. Dear Jacob, can you help me live?"

Marley only looked on sadly without reply.

"If not, what are you here for?" queried Scrooge indignantly.

"I was not sent here to fix a health problem. I was sent to point out a much greater problem – the problem with your *other* heart. Your soul is in rebellion, and tonight you get your final warning before your choice becomes an eternal one."

Scrooge did not enjoy hearing Marley make accusations against him or listening to a speech with religious overtones. "I think perhaps you *are* a hallucination, but regardless, I'm not in rebellion! Who would I be in rebellion against? God? Honestly, I'm not. I just don't believe in God – that is all. If it were reasonable to believe in God, I would."

"God is not obliged to overwhelm you with the reality of his existence. Neither is he obliged to fix your health problems. Both your knowledge and your health are *completely* gifts from Him and you have no claim to them. Consider, though, that God has not hidden himself from you; instead, it is you who ran away from him. Perhaps God has been reaching for your heart your whole life and you have been pulling away." Marley paused to let Scrooge consider his life, then continued with a sudden shout. "This is your last chance: You will be haunted by three spirits!"

"I think I'd rather not," said Scrooge.[18]

"Without their visits," said Marley, "you cannot hope to shun the path to your own destruction. You will encounter three spirits before the night's end. Listen to them, Scrooge – they look out for your welfare. They battle for your soul against the Devil who is ready to devour you."

"Oh, really? I see no evidence for the existence of God *or* the Devil. None whatsoever!" retorted Scrooge while glancing around the room as if to show to Marley that he's looking for God and the Devil and not seeing them yet.

"Who are you trying so hard to convince, dear friend?" replied Marley sadly. "I'm long dead and I see clearly now."

"*You* are a hallucination. I'm sure of it now."

Marley gave a desperate cry, "Oh, Scrooge, how I longed for you to hear my words! But rationalize me away as a hallucination, and I, with a sorrow for things unaccomplished, will oblige."

In that instant Scrooge was alone again, standing in the deathly silence, standing next to his corpse. I imagine no man has ever been so out of place in his own home. It occurred to him as he stood there, caught between life and death, that this evening was the first time in a very long time where he felt he had lost control. In fact, not since he was a boy had Scrooge really lost control.

STAVE II – THE GHOST OF CHRISTMAS PAST

After only a few moments of being alone in his room, Scrooge had the sense he was being watched. He slowly turned about the room looking to see if his feeling could be confirmed, but he could see no one and thus began to reassure himself that it was all in his head. It was only after he convinced himself of this and after he had calmed himself again that he spotted something reflected in the corner of a full length cheval mirror near the wall. A tiny, completely ugly creature was crouched in a seated position on the floor beneath his desk behind him. The creature was staring at him intently. The sight in the mirror gave Scrooge quite a start, and he spun around to be face to face with the creature.

Very unnerving! Scrooge thought.

The creature most closely resembled an elf or a troll, had large, bright eyes, and bore a caricatured resemblance to Scrooge. In one instant Scrooge thought, *I recognize myself so clearly.* But in the next instant his perception would change, and the same creature would strike him as so ugly and repulsive that he shuddered to think he had just admitted the creature looked like him.

He then inquired aloud, "Are you the spirit, sir, whose coming was foretold to me?"

"I am."

The voice was soft and gentle. Singularly low, as if instead of being so close to him, it were at a distance.

"Who and what are you?"

"I am the Ghost of Christmas Past."

"Long Past?" inquired Scrooge, observant of its dwarfish stature.

"No. Your past."[19]

Then strangely the ghost faded from sight only to reappear a moment later standing next to Scrooge. There was something so familiar, so peaceful and so surreal about the ghost's manner and speech that its ugly appearance and the strange occurrence of fading away and reappearing somewhere else hardly bothered Scrooge at all.

"Why should I believe in you? Perhaps you're a hallucination too."

"Perhaps, but perhaps this is not the relevant question to ask. You may believe in me or not, whichever pleases you more; but ask not this question again, for it changes nothing in the way we must proceed."

Scrooge, observing that the ghost would not be driven away by mere skepticism, then boldly inquired, "What business brings you here?"

"Your welfare!" said the ghost.

"I'm much obliged," Scrooge assured the ghost politely, "but I can't help thinking that a night of unbroken rest would have been more conducive to that end."

"Your reclamation, then. Take heed!"[20]

With that admonition, the ghost grabbed Scrooge's hand and as Scrooge looked toward the ghost, he noticed the ghost slowly closing his large eyes and at once the room faded away into the darkness.

***

The first thing visible to Scrooge was a dim light coming through a window. The light from the street outside shone through it, and Scrooge could make out falling snowflakes which reflected the light as they fell outside. Slowly the room came into full view. Scrooge soon realized where he was. He was home – not his current home, but his boyhood home. Being back home filled him with nostalgia. What a gift to be able to experience everything again, just as it was! Scrooge and the ghost were standing in one corner. There was an artificial Christmas tree in the middle of the room, but no presents were underneath it yet. There was staticky Christmas music playing softly on the radio in the background. A choir of voices harmonized with Nat King Cole who was singing "I'll be home for Christmas."

"Good heavens!" said Scrooge, clasping his hands together, as he looked about him. "I was raised in this place. I was a boy here!" He was conscious of a thousand odors floating in the air, each one connected with a thousand thoughts, and hopes, and joys, and cares long, long, forgotten!

"Your lip is trembling," said the ghost, gazing upon him mildly. "And what is that upon your cheek?"

Scrooge muttered, with an unusual catching in his voice, "It's a pimple. I beg you, lead me where you would."

"You remember this place?" inquired the spirit as he led Scrooge across the room.

"Remember it!" cried Scrooge with fervor, "I could walk it blindfold."

"Strange to have forgotten it for so many years!" observed the ghost.[21]

Scrooge moved throughout the room. "Our old TV, my old ant farm! Dad's old piece-of-junk cuckoo clock. He could never get it to keep time, but it sure had a lot of character." Scrooge defended the clock in a way meant to ward off criticism from the ghost. He could only bear to hear himself call the old cuckoo clock a piece of junk because he meant it as a term of endearment. Then he spotted a lamp that used an antique Black Label beer can as a part of its base. "Dad's beer can desk lamp! – even more novel than the cuckoo clock, by golly!" Everything he encountered caused him to praise it somehow. Those objects connected him to a period of his life full of unbridled joy, a period that had long since vanished. He was awash in nostalgia and had the spirit of a boy – not yet hardened by the world, but in love with every amazing thing in the world.

Suddenly, there was a noise from another room – a door slam. Scrooge's light-hearted mood vanished, and a feeling of dread swept over him.

When his father walked into the room, Scrooge could not believe his eyes. The sight of his father brought instant pain and sadness to Scrooge's heart – almost unbearable pain and sadness, yet he could no more take his eyes off his father than he could turn himself into a daisy. The feeling of having lost control that bothered him earlier returned.

Scrooge could only mutter the words, "After all these years."

His father did not respond. The Ghost of Christmas Past explained in an effort to steady Scrooge, "These are but shadows of the things that have been. They have no consciousness of us."[22]

His father, a broad shouldered man in his late thirties with a touch of gray in the temples, marched about the room in a busy, efficient manner. He carried a full suitcase which he laid on the coffee table, opened and began stuffing in yet more things, although they'd hardly fit. The look on his face was unhappy and impatient. He walked about with sudden, rushed movements looking for and picking up various objects and placing them in the suitcase.

A moment later, a boy crept down the hallway that connected the family room to the bedrooms. The boy was Ebenezer Scrooge himself. He looked afraid and sad as he spied on his father. The older Ebenezer felt the need to narrate the scene for the ghost, but could not speak. So the two of them watched silently as this shadow of Scrooge's history replayed itself.

"Daddy, why do you have to go?" called young Ebenezer from the hall.

The father's head shot up surprised. "What? ... I told you to wait in your room." He paused, then continued in a more measured tone of voice, "Son, your mother and I are getting a divorce. Sometimes mothers and father just grow apart and that's what's happened to your mother and me. Those are the breaks, kiddo. Look, I know you don't want this, but you're really too young to understand. It's nobody's fault and it may seem bad now, but don't worry – it always works out in the long run. "

"But how is it going to work out?"

"You're too young to understand."

"Well, why do you have to leave out of town?" The questions were getting tougher.

"Oh. Well. I got a friend waiting for me in Miami."

"When will I see you again?"

The father paused with a look of sheer discomfort on his face. "Soon, kiddo. We'll work something out."

"But when?"

"I'll have to figure out something with your mother, but we're not going to figure it out now anyhow." That came out in a rush, almost flippantly.

"Well, we can try." young Ebenezer responded hopefully.

"I know, but we'll have to work it out later. My ride will be here any second and I'm going to finish packing. I want you to go play in your room with your sister before she's out here too," the father added in an attempt to preempt any more delays.

"Okay, Daddy. I'll miss you so much."

"Right. Now go play with your sister." said the father almost pleading, hoping to finally end this awkward scene, but it was about to get more awkward.

"Okay," young Ebenezer conceded and turned to go, but he only got about three steps before he stopped. Then he turned back and called out desperately, "Daddy, I don't want to play. I want to be with you. Please stay!"

For a flickering moment, there seemed a hope that his father would stay, as he stood there and thought, pale faced and open mouthed. Then he frowned and turned away as he hardened in his resolve to carry out his plans. "I know, son. But I have to."

"Why?"

A honk of a horn from the driveway interrupted the conversation. The father looked out the window and thought for a moment without speaking. The taxi had come to take the father to the airport.

"To your room!' he shouted abruptly. It was the overpowering tone of voice he used to end conversations. Young Ebenezer ran down the hallway to the room where his sister was playing. The father then closed his suitcase, took one last look around the room, grabbed the beer can lamp and the cuckoo clock, laid them in a small box which he wedged under the same arm he used to hold his suitcase.

The horn honked again and the father bolted out the door.

As the door slammed shut, Scrooge turned to the ghost. "I was nine years old. I never heard from my father again." The ghost didn't respond as Scrooge fought fiercely against the emotions he felt. When he finally regained control of himself, he continued in a serious, stoic voice, "Can we go?"

The ghost nodded. "We have more we must see." It grabbed Scrooge's hand, closed his eyes, and at once the room faded away into the darkness.

***

A moment later as they re-emerged into the light, again there was Christmas music playing softly in the background. A choir of deep, bass voices sang:

"God rest ye merry gentlemen. Let nothing you dismay.
Remember Christ, our Savior, was born on Christmas day.
To save us all from Satan's power when we had gone astray.
O-oh tidings of comfort and joy, comfort and joy.
O-Oh tidings of comfort and joy."

Scrooge and the ghost were standing in the corner of a waiting room at a doctor's office. Again, it was clearly another Christmas season – the office decorated with tinsel and Christmas trinkets. Scrooge saw a shadow of himself, now a couple years older. This young man version of Scrooge was seated in a chair next to his little sister, waiting. After a moment, his mother came out of the doctor's office and approached him with a look of anguish on her face. Her eyes were red. She had been crying, no doubt, but was not crying now. Without saying a word to her children, they left. The ghost looked at Scrooge for recognition of this shadow. Scrooge obliged by narrating in a low, solemn voice, "Just an ordinary trip to the doctor's office, I thought, but my mother had just been diagnosed with cancer. My father had abandoned us a few years earlier. Why would God want to take my mother from me as well? She *had* to live. It was a very fearful time for me. I constantly thought of my mother's illness and what a horror life would be if she died." As Scrooge was talking, the ghost closed his eyes and all faded to darkness.

***

A dim light began to glow through a window. This window was stained glass. They were in the dim narthex of a church. As the light grew, one could see that the church had a domed ceiling and the walls were covered in elaborate icon paintings -- icons of biblical scenes and icons of saints. Many of the icons of saints had candles burning in front of them. In the background you could hear an old man with a haunting voice chanting quietly in Greek. Scrooge recalled the deep sense of peace this building used to convey to him. The young man Scrooge and his mother were also there. His mother lit a candle and delivered it to the foot of an icon. She signed herself with the cross with two fingers and a thumb pressed together. The two remaining fingers pressed to her palm.

The ghost asked Scrooge, "Do you remember the symbolism of the signing of the cross?"

Scrooge huffed in a disinterested manner, "Ah, I was probably sleeping during that part of catechism!"

Scrooge's mother made the sign of the cross slowly and deliberately with her head bowed. When she finished, she walked over to another icon which contained the image of Jesus, leaned forward, and kissed the feet of Jesus and crossed herself again. Finally, she returned to the young man Scrooge who had watched from a distance.

When she was close enough for him to whisper, he asked, "Who is the saint you put the candle by?"

His mother replied, "It's St. Nektarios of Aegina, the patron saint of cancer patients. I prayed for victory over cancer, if it be God's will."

"How can praying to a saint make a difference?"

His mother shrugged. "I don't know. I was taught that we can ask the saint to intercede to God for us, just as we ask our friends on Earth to pray for us. What I know for sure is that we need all the help we can get. You ought to pray too."

Young Scrooge contemplated the possibility that his prayer would go unanswered. If the cancer was not cured, his mother would die. His mother was such a great source of comfort to him. The thought of losing his mother and never seeing her again filled him with horror. The loneliness of life without her was more than this young man thought he could bear. His face was full of fear as his eyes welled up in tears. He nodded in assent to his mother's request and desperately hugged his mother. His mother quietly gave him reassurances and the two slowly left the church.

In quiet moments, later, young Scrooge would ask difficult questions like: *Why do good people die at all? If God is good, why can't he just save them and spare them the agony? Is God not all loving after all? If He is all loving, is He not all-powerful as well?* But in this moment of crisis those questions held little interest. Young Scrooge's only concern was that his mother live. If a miracle was needed, then he simply wanted God to deliver a miracle. He did not want to know anything else except that his mother would live.

Before the door of the church closed, the ghost slowly closed his eyes and the light faded to darkness for Scrooge.

***

In only a moment the time-tripping duo re-emerged into the light. They were now outdoors – apparently deep in the countryside on a hill. There was one lone tree nearby, nicely pruned, but bare. The snow was flying. The sky was gray and the wind biting and cold, but the weather made no impression on either Scrooge or the ghost. They were only seeing shadows of the past. They spotted young Scrooge at a distance standing in front of a grave with his sister by his side. This shadow was of a cemetery deep in the country. The young Scrooge looked stoic as he turned and walked away. His sister stayed a moment longer, but then turned to catch up to her brother. No speeches, no outbursts, no tears – Scrooge's face was hard with pitiless indifference. The change in his manner compared to the scene in the church was about 180 degrees and was as chilling as the driving snow. The old Scrooge was not without emotion though. He decided that if this return to the past was for his supposed benefit, he could feel free to speak his mind.

So he turned to the ghost and asked in seething anger, "Ghost, tell me what you make of this mess, please! My mother has just died. Who's in control? What kind of fool calls out for divine help? I do, that's who! But it seems pretty clear that no one's on the other end of the line to get the call. St. Nektarios, patron saint of cancer? To whom do I pray when my patron saint won't go to bat for me? Now I don't have a cancer problem. I've got a dead mother problem! How do you fix that?"

When Scrooge was finished with his outburst, the ghost replied in a kind, but confident tone, "There are two matters at hand: The first is whether or not it's possible that there are sufficient reasons for an all-good and all-powerful God to have allowed your mother to die in that way at that time in your life. The other is whether or not you're ready, even after all these years, to consider the first matter in a rational manner."

"Do you really think there's a possibility that God could have a sufficient reason? I don't!"

"I do," the ghost replied softly. "Are you ready to hear it?"

Scrooge did not reply, but looked away from the ghost in the direction of the grave. He observed the blowing wind's effect. The branches of the tree near the grave bent, shook, and twisted aimlessly. Looking past the tree to the sky he observed how gray it was. It was so many years ago. This day was the nadir of his life and now it is all so terribly real again.

The ghost spoke softly, "I can tell you loved your mother deeply." then paused, but since Scrooge did not interrupt, he continued slowly, "It is a shame, Scrooge, that you never spread that love to anyone else in your world. Your mother was a gift from God. But as such, you had *no* claim on her. Is there no one left in the world in need of your love now?"

Scrooge's fixed, angry expression made it clear that the ghost's words had not made any impression on him. "Maybe I had no claim to her as you say, but tell me why! Why did she die? Why did a supposedly loving God take her? Answer me if you even know!"

The ghost continued in a firm but compassionate tone, "We may never know His exact reason this side of eternity, but possible reasons abound and are not at all hard to imagine. If God is all good and His ultimate good and loving desire for His creation is for them to freely choose Him and to spend eternity in heaven with Him, then anything that works toward those ends is reasonable. If momentary pain and suffering cause some people to freely reject the evil in their lives and turn to God and as a result spend eternity with Him, then isn't that a sufficient reason?" The ghost then paused perhaps to see Scrooge's reaction to his question, but Scrooge was merely thinking and said nothing, so the ghost continued. "It's not even hypothetical – it's reality. History is laden with examples of pain and suffering achieving those very ends – people humbly turning to God when they hit rock bottom. Furthermore, some have even gone on to change the world." The ghost paused again to give Scrooge a chance to reply, but Scrooge stayed quiet and strangely calm. Seeing this the ghost proceeded. "You cannot fix the damage of a lost mother in this lifetime, but that is *entirely the point*. Sin ended all hope in this world. Everyone dies. No one gets out alive. There is no lasting peace to be found while embracing the world to the exclusion of God. There is one and only one path to escape – that is through repentance and forgiveness – our repentance … and our Creator's forgiveness."

Scrooge was not in the mood to listen to the ghost's sermon. "Come on! My mother was not such a bad person that she deserved to die like this. She never killed anyone; she never even cheated on her taxes. So why should she have to die? She was already a believer, after all."

The ghost waited until Scrooge made eye contact with him and then continued in the calm, gentle voice of a teacher, not in the abrasive tone of a debate opponent. "As a finite human being, your sense of justice is quite inadequate to make the call on God's behalf. And you, Scrooge, in particular are honestly quite morally warped and atrophied as much as any man. I can make it simple for you, though. If a man is on life-support and willfully disconnects himself from the machine, does he deserve to die? Of course he does. Now consider who God is. He is our creator and our sustainer. He is our life-support. When we sin, we turn our back on God. When we turn our back on God, we commit … suicide. *All* have sinned, and all have earned death, even your dear mother. But it doesn't end there. You aren't the only one who loves your mother. Her Creator loves her too. He made a plan for her to be reconciled to Him. God is not the source of evil, but He is the *solution*."

Scrooge did not answer, but simply hung his head.

The ghost continued, "Your mother may not have required pain and suffering to turn her heart to God. But did you ever consider once in the half century that has passed since this shadow that God might be trying to get someone else's attention other than your mother's?"

Again, there was no answer from Scrooge.

"What could God do to make this right in your eyes? Grant your mother a life of eternal peace and joy? He has promised exactly that. … Reunite you with your mother?" The ghost paused to see if this proposal resonated with Scrooge. When Scrooge looked up, the ghost proceeded emphatically. "He wants nothing more." Again, the ghost closed his eyes and the scene faded to black.

***

A moment later light slowly began to appear. The first thing visible to Scrooge was a dim light coming through a window – a window different from the previous windows. This window was stained glass, but it was not part of a church. In the stained glass one could make out the word "Morrell's." Slowly the room came into full view. It was a mostly empty pub, except for a few stray customers. Scrooge could remember this pub well. It was located across the street from Magdalen College, Oxford, where he completed his undergraduate studies. A group of well-dressed men – students including the young Scrooge and one professor – were entering. The young Scrooge was a young man now. The group entered the pub in a burst of energy and found their way to a large table in the corner, near where Scrooge and the ghost were sitting; the young men were laughing and talking loudly and ordering a few pints as soon as the waitress approached. Their presence dominated the pub, although their group was small. The professor, an older man, was just settling into his seat. The others slowly quieted down and turned their eyes toward him as he prepared to speak.

"I feel like you gentlemen need to get to know each other better," the professor began. "By the end of the semester, you'll have spent enough time working together. It just makes sense to do a little bonding before it all gets too crazy." This seemed like a nice gesture from the professor, and the students looked at each other and nodded. The professor continued lightly, "So who wants to go first? Does anyone want to share anything about themselves?" He then took a sip of the beer he'd just been handed and looked around the group trying to make eye contact to urge someone to speak.

Scrooge recalled this scene well. His fellow students were all fairly new acquaintances to each other so perhaps the professor's somewhat formal way of breaking the ice was appropriate. Regardless, the students all chuckled at the corniness of the professor's icebreaker, but they were all in a good mood, so one student sitting next to the young Scrooge took the bait and began to speak.

"Well, I'm an atheist!" said the student in a provocative tone of voice. "I was raised in a religious home, but it always seemed illogical to me. When I thought about it, atheism made more sense and I knew the only rational thing to do was to become an atheist."

The professor frowned a very forced frown at the student, so that all could observe that he found this sharing somehow unsatisfactory. Young Scrooge had expected the professor to chide that young man for being an atheist, but he had been quite wrong. The professor replied in a feigned exasperation in an effort to get a laugh, "Well, OF COURSE you're an atheist, boy, but what's newsworthy about that?"

The comment did get a few quiet chuckles from some of the students, while perhaps others were squirming. The professor continued in a somewhat odd, melodramatic way, "So maybe we should back up a bit here. For starters, is there anyone here who *actually* believes in God?" Then for the sake of being politically correct, he added the disclaimer, "Not that there's anything wrong with that."

After a good deal of silence and a number of heads shaking no, one student raised his hand nonchalantly, affirming that he was a believer. Scrooge whispered to the ghost knowingly, "This poor boy has no idea what he has just gotten himself into." The professor and the young man's classmates had provided good camaraderie and a few good laughs up to that point, so he had not had his guard up. Now he was exposed as the odd-man-out and in a moment he'd probably wish he hadn't raised his hand at all.

"No! Really?" shouted the professor in exaggerated surprise meant to solicit a good deal of laughter. This immediately embarrassed the young man. The professor continued, "You believe in God? Christianity too, I suppose? The whole bit?"

The nervous student nodded and Scrooge imagined he probably intended to explain things a bit, but only an unintelligible sound came out. Before the student could get one coherent word out, the professor's sense of comedic timing spurred him to continue quickly with the cross examination, "Why, that means you believe in talking snakes then too – Adam and Eve and the terrible talking snake! Isn't that right?"

The group of students' laughter hit a new high. The one who had raised his hand panicked and stammered, "No!" Everything was funny to the group now, so they laughed at the young man's denial too.

The ghost looked over to the old Scrooge and sadly explained, "That student wasn't at all sure how to explain what he knew, but deep down he really did believe. But in order to relieve the pain of embarrassment in this situation he impetuously decided to start conceding parts of the Bible were perhaps unbelievable ... like the talking snake part."

At this point, the old Scrooge noticed something strange about the young man -- he began to remind him of the boy that had approached him as a fan on the street on his walk home. Namely, he looked insecure and needy, and his voice had an overcompensating tone meant to mask how insecure and hurt he was. Remembering how he had humiliated the young man on the street earlier, the whole scene left Scrooge feeling a little sick to his stomach.

The professor continued condescendingly, "It's OK, boy. You go on believing it. I think it's nice. It doesn't make a bit of sense to me, but if it gets you through the night, then by all means keep the faith!" Then turning to the rest of the group, he continued, "How about the rest of you? Any of you lads believers? How about you, Ebenezer?"

The young Ebenezer Scrooge was too clever to repeat the mistakes of the first two students who had both, in different ways, embarrassed themselves. Young Ebenezer was an atheist and he felt confident that he knew why, and that made him special.

He seized the moment and launched into a diatribe. "Anyone who believes in the God of the Bible has a pathology of the mind. Religion is the opium of the simple-minded masses![23] The God of the Old Testament is an insecure, ego-driven child – demanding to be worshipped, but hardly worthy of it. But infinitely worse than a child – more like a cold-hearted, murderous tyrant and an unforgiving, merciless, contemptable dictator in the sky. One could do no greater service to mankind than to send him back to the land of make-believe from which he came."

The rhetoric was bold and haughty. The group was in awed silence until one of young Scrooge's classmates patted him on the back and joked, "Don't hold back, man. Just let us know how you really feel."

Another student chimed, "That sounds a little harsh, but you have to admit in the end that he's right."

On and on the affirmations came. The Ghost of Christmas Past turned to the old Scrooge and commented, "The boy who had raised his hand as a believer in God was quite sure he had dropped to the bottom of the pecking order of this particular group. It would be a long semester for him. But enough about him. What about you, Scrooge? Didn't those affirmations feel good? Truth be told, your pride was growing with every compliment you received and your longing for more affirmations was growing stronger by the moment."

But as the conversation amongst the students and the professor wandered to other topics, the ghost led Scrooge away to the other side of the pub to listen to three older gentlemen who had overheard the young Scrooge and the others.

"What a ghastly tirade that was, eh?" asked the first man in a loud, irritated voice. "The truth is – all of the slanders that schoolboy makes against God reflects a warped, sorry understanding of that sacred text! He'd have his naive classmates believe that faith in a loving God is the opium of the masses, but how much more has he just shown that prideful rebellion from God is the opium of the *asses*!"

All three men laughed heartily, clinked glasses, and drank.

The second man sat back and pondered the scene before them. "I wonder what that young man would have to say about the book of Jonah. That's a clear view of the true Old Testament God for you!"

"How do you mean?" asked the first.

As the second man replied, Scrooge wondered because of the way he spoke if he might be a don at the college. "The prophet Jonah hated the people of Nineveh and wanted God to punish them for their evil. Instead, God told Jonah to urge them to repent, turn to God, and be forgiven! Jonah was reluctant to do anything that might spare them from what they had coming because he despised these people. But after some supernatural persuasion, he did what God asked – he commanded them to repent. These evil people did repent, and God spared them from destruction. In chapter four Jonah is bemoaning the fact that God had spared the Ninevites. The verse goes something like this, 'But to Jonah this seemed very wrong, and he became angry. He prayed to the Lord, "I knew that you are a gracious and compassionate God, slow to anger and abounding in love, a God who relents from sending calamity."'"

"*Quod est demonstravit!*"[24] interrupted the third man.

An incredulous Scrooge turned to the ghost and exclaimed, "Talking Latin in a pub? Definitely a don ... a nerdy one."

The third man continued his comments, "Even though it didn't please Jonah at the time, we see the God of the Old Testament clearly displaying his love and compassion!"

"Yes, indeed," agreed the second man, "and that's my point. It's not a secret – it's on display in the book of Jonah. Before anyone condemns the God of the Old Testament, perhaps they might bother reading it?"[25]

"Or if he's read it," the first man returned, "maybe he's just got his own interpretation of the words. Perhaps he's straining a wee-bit on the exegesis?"

"More like eisegesis, if you ask me. I suppose if you strain hard enough, you can invent your own preferred meaning. But that young man is either straining like he's giving birth or he doesn't know the story."

The third man nodded. "Agreed! I'd call his rant sophomoric, but I'm afraid that would be insulting to sophomores. One thing's for certain after watching that young man's tirade -- education without values seems rather to make man a more clever devil."[26] Then he continued in a more serious tone. "And there's also the problem of his pride -- it can grow into a terrible addiction. I feel like I'm seeing it take root in that young man right there. I fear that God will not force him into heaven against his will. And it seems to me that this boy's pride has him racing down a road that leads far away from God. God have mercy on him."

With that the three men nodded to each other and with a hint of solemnity clinked their pint glasses again.

Scrooge turned to the ghost. "I get it. Let me summarize: 'I'm prideful, so don't listen to me.' They don't have any inkling of what they're talking about. What about the other places in the Old Testament where God acts so evil?"

The ghost looked at Scrooge steadily. "When you say God acts evil, you assume there's good. When you assume there's good, you assume there's such a thing as a moral law on the basis of which to differentiate between good and evil. But if you assume a moral law, you must posit a moral Law Giver, but that's Who you're trying to disprove and not prove. Because if there's no moral Law Giver, there's no moral law. If there's no moral law, there's no good. If there's no good, there's no evil. What is your question?"[27]

Not liking to be made a fool of by the ghost, Scrooge lashed out, "I'd like to punch them in the nose. They're foul mouthed, ignorant old bums – getting drunk in a pub no less. Am I supposed to listen to them?"

"They don't seem drunk to me, but I'm sorry it wasn't St. Peter and St. Paul sitting near you in the pub. The fact is, you've already listened to them. Why not consider what they say? Does the source of the information determine whether the information is true? If you gave me a fact, like 2+2 = 4, a fact that you knew was true, and I inserted it into a fortune cookie, gave you the fortune cookie, and you then opened the fortune cookie and read 2+2 = 4, would that change the truth value of the equation? After all, nobody believes what they read in fortune cookies, right? The credibility of the source *determines* the truthfulness of the message, right? No, 2+2 = 4 is still true even if you learn about it from a fortune cookie. Similarly, if there's truth being shared by these men, as flawed as they might be, does what you think of them change the truth of what they're saying?

"The message of the Old Testament is that God is clearly a God of justice, but no less a God of mercy and love. The truth of the matter can be determined by a sophisticated technique that scholars call *reading*.[28] Read the Bible yourself, dear Scrooge, as these 'ignorant bums' have done, and look past your *prima facie* impressions before you pass judgment. God's mercy and love ring loud and clear in the Old Testament histories of Jonah, Abraham, Joseph, David, and in the countless times God called the people of Israel to repent from their wrongdoing so that they could enjoy their Creator's forgiveness and love. Sorry, the tirade of young Scrooge does not ring true."

At the moment the ghost reached his conclusion, Scrooge lunged in the direction of the ghost, extending his hand toward the ghosts face in order to cover the ghost's eyes, saying, "Enough of your visions!" Scrooge fell short though and collapsed to the ground. Regardless of his failed attempt to control the situation, the visions of the past faded into the darkness.

STAVE III – THE GHOST OF CHRISTMAS PRESENT

Scrooge found himself on the ground in his bedroom again. He glanced under the desk where the ghost had first appeared to him, but the Ghost of Christmas Past was nowhere to be seen. The ghost had not even said goodbye. Scrooge's corpse was still there though, quite cold by now Scrooge imagined. The sight repulsed and saddened him.

With the sight of his corpse combined with all the fresh images of his past, Scrooge felt overwhelmingly depressed, so alone in his room. He could hardly muster the energy to cry. His despair would have continued longer no doubt, but it was interrupted abruptly by the housekeeper opening the door and entering the room. She had been Scrooge's housekeeper for many, many years. Scrooge always called her Mrs. Garrett, in reference to the maid on the TV show, *Diff'rent Strokes*, which had been popular when she first started. Scrooge had pulled that name out of the air to rescue himself from an awkward moment in her first days of work when she had greeted him by name, and he, being notoriously forgetful of names, had replied, "Good morning to you, …, uh, Mrs. Garrett." She had given a polite laugh, which

Scrooge had taken as a sign that the nickname was a success and continued to use it. Now, though, he wondered briefly whether she disliked the nickname after all these years, perhaps had disliked it from the very beginning. All Scrooge knew was that she was a somewhat distant, but very effective and seemingly loyal housekeeper, who knew Scrooge so well after all these years that she could practically read his mind. Tonight she was delivering a blanket to his room knowing that he'd probably be cold at some point in the night, but upon seeing Scrooge's body lying on the floor, she gave a little scream. Scrooge's hope soared. He had been discovered. Now possibly he could be saved and this nightmare might end.

She then approached the body asking aloud, "Dr. Scrooge, are you all right?" Upon one touch she recoiled and exclaimed, "Ice cold!" She then paused and looked around. A moment later she was cleaning out Scrooge's cash which was hidden in his dresser. "Won't be needing this." she thought aloud.

A glaring buzz rang out and she straightened herself quickly in response. To Scrooge her reaction looked like a burglar tripping an alarm. But in only a moment she regained her composure. Scrooge realized it was only a coincidental ring of the doorbell.

"Very strange," she thought aloud as she glanced out the window, "to have a visitor to the house so late at night on Christmas Eve." She quickly exited the bedroom leaving with the money in her pocket and closing the door behind her.

Scrooge was irate. Why hadn't Mrs. Garrett done anything to help him? How could she have been so heartless -- stealing from what she thought was a dead man? She had no honor. What she had done was pure treachery. Scrooge swelled with feelings of righteous indignation, but his thoughts were interrupted by the sound of laughter, a deep, full laughter that grew louder and began to echo off the walls. It was coming from the small room adjacent to Scrooge's bedroom.

While the laughter was strange and powerful, it hardly fazed Scrooge at all. He had had quite a night already having collapsed on his floor, met his dead friend Marley, and met the first yuletide specter. I don't mind telling you that by now he was ready for a good broad field of strange appearances, and that nothing between a baby and rhinoceros would have astonished him very much.[29] So Scrooge, almost beyond fear and shock, rose and made his way to the adjoining room. The moment Scrooge's hand was on the lock, the strange voice called him by his name, and invited him to enter. He obeyed.

The room he was entering was a neglected spare room. But it had undergone a surprising transformation. The walls and ceiling were hung with living green and from every part of it bright gleaming berries glistened. The crisp leaves of holly, mistletoe, and ivy reflected back the light, as if so many little mirrors had been scattered there. And the most astonishing of the decorations, a Christmas tree, had sprouted and reached to the ceiling, beaming with colored lights that were right out of some yuletide fairytale with a preternatural brightness and beauty beyond what Scrooge had ever imagined. Before the tree stood a couch that Scrooge had replaced long ago but never bothered to throw out, its worn upholstery transformed to be like new and sporting a cheerful red and green tapestry. In a comfortable pose upon this couch sat a jolly giant, glorious to see. To Scrooge the ghost looked something like a primitive version of Father Christmas. He wore neither black boots nor red stocking cap, but bare feet, a green hooded cloak, and a wreath of holly instead. He bore a glowing torch, in shape like Plenty's horn. He held it high up to shine its light on Scrooge, as Scrooge peeped from behind the door.

"Come in!" exclaimed the ghost. "Come in and know me better, man!"

Scrooge entered timidly and hung his head before this spirit. Although the spirit's eyes were clear and kind, Scrooge was reluctant to look him in the eyes. In the background he could hear Christmas music playing. The chords were familiar, but the sound was distant and had a ghostly echo. The eerie remix gave Scrooge a dread sense that his time with this ghost would not be to his liking.

"I am the Ghost of Christmas Present," said the spirit as he stood and stepped toward Scrooge.[30] Then, noticing Scrooge's bemused expression, he exclaimed, "You have never seen the likes of me before!"

"Never."

"Have you never walked forth with my elder brothers born in these later years?"

"I don't think I have," said Scrooge. "Have you had many brothers, spirit?"

"More than two thousand," exclaimed the ghost with a smile.

"A tremendous family to provide for."

The ghost laughed but then switched to a most serious expression and commanded, "Touch my robe!"

Scrooge did as he was told, and held it fast.[31] Away the two flew at such a great speed that to Scrooge all images were reduced to a blur of light, then all was black and quiet.

***

The first thing Scrooge was aware of was the sound of a grandfather clock ringing out the sounds of twelve midnight. A room came into view, first the lights of a Christmas tree, then the rest of the room. There, relaxing together on the sofa next to a modest Christmas tree, were a man in his late forties, relatively short and thin, and a woman who looked a few years younger, with dark hair with streaks of gray and ageless beauty. They sat shoulder to shoulder, facing the tree and talking. Everything in the room had an aged look about it. It would have been difficult to imagine the Christmas decorations, the blankets, the furniture, the clock or anything in the room as ever having been new. They were not broken or worn out, but all bore the signs of years of use. There were no precious heirlooms or antiques – nothing that would be cried over if broken, nothing too costly to replace. The focal point of the room was the tree; its lights glowed bright, reflecting off of the ornaments in the otherwise darkened room.

"What a dumpy apartment," Scrooge commented.

"Let me say this in their defense – there's nothing here

anymore dumpy than an old beer can desk lamp."

Scrooge's face reddened at the ghost's reference to the beloved lamp that he had witnessed in the vision from the past. The ghost directed Scrooge to listen to the conversation between the couple which was already in progress.

"Why are we here, kind sir?" Scrooge asked the ghost with feigned politeness. "I don't even know these people. And honestly, I have no interest in eavesdropping on their holiday conversation."

The ghost did not reply but looked on and listened to their conversation. Worry had crept into the woman's eyes.

"What's the problem?" the man said jokingly. "Your husband's apparently one of the most wanted men in the country. Doesn't every family need a black sheep? Why can't it be me?"

She shook her head. "I can't think about it, or it will be too much. What if they arrest you? I can't bear the thought of you in prison and the children without their father."

The man turned his gaze from the woman. Rather than deny the possibility, he began to philosophize with a far off look, "After World War II, many dads didn't come home because they had sacrificed all for a cause much greater than themselves, but the father's impact on the family didn't fade because the father's physical presence faded. In fact, it was often amplified through the efforts of his wife, who made sure their father's legacy was understood and never forgotten, but instead something to be cherished and lived up to. Their sacrifice and integrity was immortalized and permanently imbedded in the hearts and minds of the family members left behind. That's...." The man's voice trailed off for a moment. "That's not the storyline I want for our family, but if it's a worst case scenario, then it's a scenario I can be at peace with."

"I'm so tired of being in a culture war that we didn't ask to be a part of, but I trust your judgment, and I know you've done what's right."

"I love you." He paused a moment, then took a deep breath and patted her knee with a smile. "Let's get some rest. It's after midnight already – it's actually Christmas – Merry Christmas then. But let's get to bed, since it will be morning soon."

With that, the man stood up and walked out of the room. The woman lingered for a moment, though, and reached to check her cell phone. Still bored, Scrooge tried to get a glimpse of the tiny screen and finally managed it when she set the phone down with a heavy, worried sigh. She had no voice or text messages and no missed calls. "Celebrating reason this season with Scrooge," she muttered to herself in disbelief.

Scrooge was modestly interested now that he was part of the storyline. "Whatever does that mean? Who is celebrating with me and why?"

The ghost explained the scene for Scrooge, "With all that is on her husband's mind, she can't bear to share yet one more burden with him. She had an argument with her son about his new found doubts about the church earlier today. She feels responsible for how the conversation ended which involved the son storming off. This problem is one she feels she must bear and solve herself."

The woman spoke softly to herself. "Bob can't be the black sheep in the family. We already have Peter. Time to go looking for the lost sheep." With that thought on her lips, she grabbed her phone and coat, found her keys, and went out the door.

"Now where's she going?" Scrooge said with irritation in his voice.

As the woman emerged in her car from the apartment building's parking structure, the man re-emerged from the bedroom, frowning. "Emily? Where are you?" He spotted her car in the street below as she drove away. He grabbed his phone and quickly called her. When she picked up, he asked, "Where on earth are you going in the middle of the night?"

Scrooge could barely hear her sigh over the tiny cell phone earpiece. "I didn't want to burden you with another problem, dear, but Peter and I had a fight today and now he hasn't come home. I'm going to find him to make sure he's all right."

"I don't want you cruising the streets at this time of night, either. Now I've got to worry about you and him."

"Don't worry about either of us. I think I know where he is. I'm pretty sure he went to see Dr. Scrooge. You stay with the kids. I can fix this. I'll be home shortly. Bye!" And she hung up.

The ghost commented again, "It's not lost on Bob that his son, Peter, shares so much in common with his mother, Emily. Both are very strong willed, determined to make up their own minds and to do so in often a manner that can be trying on those closest to them."

Scrooge, who was barely paying attention to the words of the ghost, snorted in amusement. "The father must feel like an idiot to not even have known until that moment that his son was missing." Still, Scrooge now knew the names of those involved – Emily, Bob, and their runaway son, Peter.

Bob thought for a moment before springing into action himself, running into the kids' bedrooms. "Kids! Wake up. Wake up! We need to go. I need you to get up. Please get up and get into the van."

Drowsy and confused, two younger children, a boy and a girl, emerged from their rooms, whining questions Scrooge didn't quite understand.

"We just got an urgent message from Peter," Bob continued. "He spotted Santa and his sleigh spilled hundreds of presents into the snow. It will be hours before his elves can get there to help clean up. We've got to find Peter and Santa and save Christmas!"

"Where's Mommy?" were the first words out of the half-awake boy.

"She's already out there helping Peter."

"But I'm sleepy, and my knee hurts."

"It's just growing pains, Tim," Bob replied hurriedly. "Come on, let's go."

The girl helped her little brother out of the house, steadying him as he limped.

"This little one's like a 'little mommy' to her brother," the ghost informed Scrooge, pointing to Martha as they followed Bob and his children out to the apartment building's parking structure. "Martha gave up hope that Santa was real years ago, but she trusts that her father has an unspoken, good reason for what they're doing. And she knows better than to spoil the fun for Tiny Tim. Peter does that enough already, and she sees how it hurts Tim more clearly than he does.

"You had a younger sister who had passed away as a young mother giving birth to your nephew, Fred. You two were not terribly close during her life and you always preferred the company of adults." the ghost observed. Scrooge's face reddened as he listened to the recounting of these personal details about his relationship with his late sister. He then watched bemusedly as Martha helped Tim into the van and made sure he was settled comfortably before buckling in herself. Martha was breaking the stereotype he held of young children – that they were all self-centered, at least as self-centered as he remembered being at that age.

Once all three were in the car Bob addressed his children, "I'd like you both to fold your hands and bow your heads for a quick prayer before we start this journey." Both children granted their father's request and Bob began, "Dear Heavenly Father, thank you for Christmas. Thank you for this little adventure we're going on now. Keep us safe as we travel the streets tonight. Please bless us, Lord, on our journey. Amen."

Keeping his head down and hands folded, Tim, now awake, implored, "God, please keep Santa safe. And God bless us, everyone!"[32] Bob smiled and drove off into the darkness of the first hour of Christmas Day.

The ghost turned to Scrooge to summarize the scene, "Just a terribly common sort of family, living with hardship and in apparent chaos, it seems. But even in the chaos, there's a peace about the family that is very uncommon ... and dare I say very attractive. The mother looking out for her son, the father looking out in turn for his wife, and not least of all the little girl watching out for her even littler brother."

Scrooge, so fiercely independent since losing his mother, wondered again what it would be like to let someone take care of him again. Yet there wasn't time for him to ponder it for long. As the Cratchit van disappeared down the road, the ghost and Scrooge disappeared into the night as well.

***

First the brightness of morning hit Scrooge's eyes; then images began to come into focus. The first image Scrooge could make out was that of a church building rapidly approaching. Scrooge and the ghost were high over the city, descending like birds upon the church roof. But they did not come to rest there. Instead they passed on through the roof into the mighty sanctuary of the huge, historic First Evangelical Church. The ghost flew triumphantly high through the air in the open space of the sanctuary, pulling Scrooge along with him. The sanctuary, which was of a beautiful baroque architecture, decorated with greenery, red ribbons, and lights for Christmas, was brimming with life. The organist was pounding out "Oh Come, All Ye Faithful" as the enormous crowd below was in motion. It was Christmas morning after all. There were those leaving from a service just completed and those filing in for the next service. The church was brimming with smiles, activity, and excitement. Warm, multi-colored light poured in through the stained glass windows that stretched from a few feet above the floor to within a few feet of the arched ceiling. The ghost and Scrooge listed to and fro above the congregation as if gently swayed by a breeze, the ghost reveling in the moment, but even the gentle sway was most disconcerting to Scrooge. Scrooge and the ghost passed unseen from the sanctuary into the narthex and down a wide, old staircase that led to an area in the basement of the church known as the undercroft, which was used for large meetings and events. In the undercroft, many young children were being dropped off by their parents for Sunday School. Those that had been dropped off were clustering around and clinging to their Sunday School teachers, who were waiting for the rest of the students to arrive so that the program could begin. Also in the undercroft was Fred. He was seated amongst the three-year-old Sunday School class with his daughter, who was too afraid to be in Sunday School without one of her parents.

In a matter of moments, a lady came forward with a

microphone and announced, "Merry Christmas everyone. Mr. Toppolowski has agreed to teach the three-year-old through kindergarten classes today, but he hasn't arrived yet." She grimaced, which got a few giggles from the little ones as if they knew it was a joke, and requested, "Everyone please remain patient for just a moment longer."

No sooner had she gone back to her seat when in wandered the most aimless, confused looking man. He was a young man in his late twenties with a wiry build and hair that looked not merely uncombed, but more like it had either encountered electricity or a windstorm. He was open mouthed and wide eyed. It was an expression a three year old could instinctively recognize as very, very silly. As he passed by the children he said, "I'm looking for Sunday School. Can anyone help me find Sunday School? I'm so lost! Can you help me?"

The children were instantly transfixed by the newcomer. Those closest to him began to shout, "Here! Here! This is Sunday School. You found it!"

But the man seemed not to hear them and kept asking his questions louder, sounding more forlorn by the moment. "Where, *oh* where is Sunday School?"

He made his way to the front of the room and the lady who had just spoken on the microphone rose again from her seat and began to encourage the children to quiet down and listen, though now more and more of them where joining in the chorus of, "This is Sunday School! You found it!"

Then as the man reached the front of the room the lady spoke to him, as if acting out a skit. "Excuse me, sir. What's your name?"

The man replied, "I'm Topper."

"OK, Topper. Merry Christmas to you. This is Sunday School. How can we help you?"

"Merry Christmas! I'm looking for Sunday School and I'm so lost."

The kids were screaming in laughter. Hadn't he just been told he was in Sunday School? What a confused, silly man.

Then in a loud voice, meant to be heard by all, Fred called out from the middle of the three-year-old group, "Topper! This is Sunday School. You're here. The real question is, what are you doing here?"

"Oh, a very good question indeed. I can tell you: I like Sunday School very much. It's my favorite part of Wednesday."

The kids screamed with laughter at the man's latest mistake and Fred stood up from his seat and started to walk to the front to join in the fun, grinning from ear to ear. Seeing that Fred was taking charge of the situation, the lady with the microphone gave the children a wink and sat down.

Once at the front of the room, Fred declared, "Sunday School is on Sunday, not Wednesday. They call it Sunday School because it happens on Sunday."

"Oh, is that why there were no people here last time?" Topper shook his head. "I just thought this church had really bad Sunday School attendance. Anyway, I like to *teach* Sunday School. Will you let me teach?"

"What do you know about God? If you tell us what you know, then maybe we can decide if you're fit to teach. Personally, I have my doubts."

"Well, I know about Christmas. And the, um, *seven* wise men."

"You mean the *three* wise men?"

"The guys that visited baby Jesus? I'm pretty sure there's seven. I counted them just before I got here." Then turning to the kids, Topper asked, "How many wise men are there?"

The kids shouted back, "THREE!"

"Oh, I don't know. Let's count them." He then wander over to a Nativity scene under a Christmas tree at the front of the room and began to count slowly, picking up each one and showing it to the kids as he counted, "One, f-four, … seven."

The kids laughed and shouted, "No! No! Two comes after one!"

On and on the comedy of errors continued. Topper suggested, "The wise men brought baby Jesus gifts of gold, franks and beans, and myrrh," but the kids were quick to point out in a chorus of shouts that franks and beans was very wrong as well. The kids were in a frenzy from beginning to end. Scrooge was amazed at how funny they found Topper and how tireless they were in correcting and helping this hapless man. He was also amazed at how shamelessly long Topper was willing to milk each shtick, making sure to go for every last laugh. When Sunday School was nearly finished, Topper led them all on his guitar with a rousing version of "We *Three* Kings" although Topper sang it as "we seven kings" instead – just for fun.

Finally Topper led them in a short prayer. "Dear God, we just want to say Happy Birthday to Your Son, Jesus. It's so awesome that we get presents on Jesus' birthday. Wow. But we're the most thankful for the greatest gift of all that You gave us, Your Son, Jesus, who died for our sins. And we thank You also for Your promise to take us to the greatest place ever, Your home in heaven. God – we love You. Amen."

"AMEN!" cried all of the children at once.

After the Sunday Schoolers were dismissed, Topper and Fred sat down to talk. The Ghost of Christmas Present led Scrooge up close to them to listen.

"Nice job, buddy," Fred said still grinning. "Very entertaining, but did you actually teach the kids anything?"

Topper grimaced, realizing he had gotten lost in the moment. But when Fred laughed, Topper thought a moment, then said in his defense, "Reviewing is teaching, right?"

"Fair enough. You were great. You're a born clown."

"That's true."

"Are you still planning to come over tonight for the Christmas party?"

"Yeah, I'll be there. Thanks for asking. It's a generous invitation. My family is so spread out that we typically don't get together until the weekend after Christmas, so I don't usually have anything special going on Christmas Day."

"Hey, you know you're always welcome. You're the life of the party. I just wish the Cratchits could come; I think they could all use a good laugh. Have you noticed Pastor Bob's been a bit down lately?"

"I haven't had a chance to talk with him, honestly. I know he's in a heap of trouble over the hate speech law, but I haven't heard how he's handling it."

"It has to be tough on him and his family. I wish there was something we could do for him – to help him in his fight against Scrooge's law or just to help lift his spirits."

"Well, if you think of something, count me in. I heard a rumor the LWLs are going to start picketing our church building, publicizing member names to the media, outing us as bigots, pressuring our employers to fire us, … that sort of thing. It could get rough for all of us if that happens."

"Yup. Imagine fighting your way past rowdy protestors just to get to Bible class. Imagine choosing between keeping our job and following your conscience. When I was a kid, I thought church was dull, but I'd gladly take the dull when you consider the drama we could all be in for if those rumors turn out to be true."

"I don't even want to think about it. Listen, I have to go. I'll see you tonight. Oh, is your uncle gonna be at your party?"

"Uncle Scrooge? Not likely, but he's invited, so you never know."

"Celebrating Christmas with the king of Grinches. That would be memorable!" Topper laughed as he turned to the staircase.

The ghost held Scrooge by the arm and they followed, but Topper quickly disappeared in plain sight.

***

As the ghost led Scrooge through the building, Scrooge could tell by the shifting light in the windows that the day was progressing rapidly. Hours of Christmas Day were passing in mere seconds as they moved up the old staircase and through the narthex. Through a side door they glided, then down a dim hallway that led to the church offices. Finally, they landed gently and passed through a closed door into the head pastor's office.

The old clock on the wall showed that it was now 1 p.m. There they found two people meeting at a large wooden table in a spacious office, a man dressed as a pastor, and a sharply dressed woman reviewing her notes and setting a recording device on the table. Scrooge looked more closely at the man's face and declared, "Why, it's the man from the other shadow! Is he a pastor? Did he ever find his son? Was his son with me? And who is this woman? Do I know her?"

"You'll know *all* in due time, but for now it will suffice to tell you the names of these two. The woman is Marissa Hessen, the journalist to whom you and your lawyers gave the interview yesterday. The other?" The ghost paused a moment. "The other is Bob Cratchit, the man whom you persecute."

"Is this the pastor who is to be charged according to the new hate speech legislation? If so, I don't think I persecute him, really. He persecutes himself by choosing to engage in hate speech. I have no responsibility for what happens to that man," declared Scrooge sanctimoniously.

The ghost did not reply but was already staring intently on the shadow of the two people at the table and listening to their conversation. Realizing the ghost was not willing to debate the matter, Scrooge quickly began to listen, too.

"I'm glad you're here," said Bob, smiling genially. "It's a real show of integrity and commitment to good journalism that you'd take the time to get both sides of the story."

"Thanks," Ms. Hessen replied, not returning the smile. "I take my work seriously. I apologize for setting this meeting on Christmas Day, but I think we both recognize the urgent nature of things. I'm eager to complete this story, so let's get started. What is your understanding of the law that's been passed?"

"I'm not a lawyer, but I think the law says that I can't condemn the practices of the Love Without Limits community or it will be considered hate speech. Is that right?"

Ms. Hessen ignored Bob's request for confirmation and kept her eyes down as she reviewed her notes. She then asked, "What do you think is at stake for you and your church if you are charged under this legislation and lose the case?"

"It's my understanding that I could be imprisoned for many years and face fines that I cannot afford, and my church could lose its tax-exempt status and face devastating fines as well."

Ms. Hessen looked up to ask her next question. "Do you have a family?

"I have a wife and three children."

"You have a wife and three kids to take care of, and you could go to jail for a long time. The children would grow up without you. Also, this could financially ruin your church. Do you think this is fair?"

The unfeeling tone in her voice and the unflinching stare made the question sound almost antagonistic. Bob put both hands to his mouth and drew a deep breath as the emotions provoked by the question rolled over him. After releasing his breath, he looked back at his interviewer and replied back, "Do *you* think it's fair?"

She thought for a moment whether to answer the question, then reached forward and hit the stop button on the recorder. And thus ended the official portion of the interview. Then she leaned forward, almost whispering rather than shouting, but spoke clearly and with conviction. "Off the record, I don't think it's fair. I think you're *getting off easy*. You know the law; you know the consequences; and yet you feel like you can abuse your power as the leader of a large group of committed followers to spread hate and intolerance while innocent people are physically attacked. And while not every LWL-phobic speech causes violence, it always creates pain and division between LWLs and the rest of the community. Your type are bulls in a china shop, and it's time someone put you back in your cage."

Bob soaked in Ms. Hessen's barbed comments, took another deep breath, and replied, "I really respect what you think, and I want to understand your point of view. Human history is full of examples where hate speech and discrimination took a huge human toll."

"Yes, they have indeed."

"I don't approve of it when I see it in other people, and I certainly don't like to be accused of it. But perhaps I'm blind and don't see the true nature of what I'm doing. Perhaps you could allow me to ask you a few questions in the spirit of helping me understand what you understand."

Ms. Hessen gave an irritated huff, then a forced smile. "Well, I suppose I have time to answer a couple of questions."

"I hope I don't insult you by starting with such a basic question," Bob began, "but do you believe there's such a thing as objective right and wrong? When I say objective, I'm merely referring to something that exists independent of people's opinions. For example, is it objectively wrong to discriminate against innocent people, or is it open to each person to decide for himself? Or for another example: Hitler murdered the weak and Mother Teresa saved the weak. Was one of them truly, objectively wrong and one right, or were they acting out mere preferences? What do you say?"

She replied confidently, "Some things are really wrong. Discrimination is really, objectively wrong -- like discriminating against someone just because he's an LWL is *really* wrong."

"Great, I agree with you. That is to say, we both acknowledge there is objective right and wrong. We're off to a great start. What do we do, though, when two people in a specific instance disagree on what that objective right and wrong are – like when two people disagree about whether someone's comments are right or wrong?"

"I just fight for the side I think is right. That's what the LWLs are doing, and that's what this legislation is all about. This legislation is about right triumphing over wrong."

Without missing a beat, but without changing his gracious manner Bob replied, "So if someone thinks her point of view is right, then by your standard she is justified in fighting not merely to have her ideas be heard, but to *silence* the voice of those who disagree. Isn't that what this legislation does? It punishes anyone who speaks against the point of view ordained in the legislation, right?"

Ms. Hessen did not respond. In contrast, the ghost did react by elbowing Scrooge and nodding in agreement in the direction of the pastor with a knowing smile.

Bob continued, "Your approach, silencing the opposition, puts you in the same company as Adolf Hitler. Hitler prided himself on his ruthlessness and treachery in silencing those who opposed him. I read recently one commentator call this legislation that I'm now accused of violating the 'Kristallnacht's Eve' bill, meaning it could be a pre-cursor to events similar to those of Kristallnacht."[33]

"Now wait; that's ridiculous. Our cause is totally different from any cause that Hitler stood for."

"Perhaps, but I'm not yet weighing the merits of your cause. I'm weighing the tactics you've used to advance your cause."

"Well, you're just misrepresenting me. I would not advocate silencing the voice of dissent in just any circumstance, only when the opposing side is first showing intolerance, like those who are intolerant against the LWLs. This puts the legislation in question in a different category from Hitler completely. It only silences those who demonstrate intolerance. Intolerance is one standard that no one should violate; therefore, one is justified in silencing the intolerant."

Bob's tone remained kind, but he was clearly a little disappointed in the sloppy reasoning of his interviewer. "Unless I'm mistaken, your claim appears to be self-defeating. Wouldn't it be *intolerant* to hold the view that 'intolerance is the one standard that no one should violate?' Are you not showing intolerance to those who hold a different view? In other words, if I hold the view that intolerance should be tolerated in some instances and you do not tolerate my view, then *you* are being intolerant. You violate your own standard. Taking your view to its logical conclusion, others would be justified in silencing *you*."

At this the ghost burst out laughing. He doubled over ungracefully trying to contain his mighty laugh. When Scrooge did not react, the ghost, intent on making sure Scrooge noticed his merriment, gave Scrooge a jolly, but forceful slap on the back.

This was terribly unpleasant for Scrooge, who winced and nodded in acknowledgment that he was in fact paying attention.

Ms. Hessen, not yet absorbing the logic, responded defiantly, "The simple fact is that the LWL community and their supporters are committed to silencing those who disagree with the LWL lifestyle, and I'm fine with that."

"But by your standard of tolerance, the LWL should be silenced. In general, anyone who holds this view of tolerance is immediately in violation of his own view and is figuratively sawing off the very branch they're sitting on. Let's make a deal – we'll both tolerate views different than our own. And when I say tolerate, I mean I may strongly disagree, but I will fight for your right to say it all in the name of tolerance and in the name of free speech."

The pastor had spoken kindly, not trying to mock the interviewer, but in the eyes of the ghost the reporter was absolutely a laughing stock. At Bob's line, "sawing off the very branch they're sitting on," the ghost began a gentle laugh that Scrooge quickly acknowledged in order to avoid a repeat of the previous unpleasantness.

"Never mind tolerance," Ms. Hessen huffed. "For all I care, you can call me intolerant, but this law is still a good and necessary thing because hate speech against the LWLs is wrong."

"I actually agree that hate speech is wrong and harmful, but your prescription for fixing it silences free speech. Ironically, in asserting your opinion you make use of free speech, the very right you're OK stripping from others. You've already conceded that true right and wrong do exist, but this hate speech law cannot be a good thing because it sabotages the pursuit of truth by pre-emptively silencing one side of the debate. Rather than silencing those that disagree with you, the moral and courageous thing to do would be to engage intellectually in the issue and battle those you disagree with rhetorically. Raise the intellectual and moral price tag for them to hold their view by putting forth a well-reasoned argument that challenges their perspective, but above all *allow them to respond*. Do you think we've made society better by silencing moral speech? If moral speech can be silenced for any reason, how would one speak out against the likes of Hitler? What this all boils down to is that you can't take away the right of another person to dissent and still claim the moral or intellectual high ground."

The ghost began to commentate to Scrooge, "The reporter has only been half listening to the pastor's response, noticing the décor of his office – so many theological books and decorations. It strikes her as odd that his defense hadn't involved quoting the Bible chapter and verse up to this point."

When the pastor stopped speaking, the silence took her by surprise. Without missing a beat though she continued, "I'll never agree with you if you intend to sanction hate speech. Pastor, what about when people use free speech to incite violence? We can't have totally free speech and protect people from violence at the same time."

"Again, I agree with you. It's not conducive to living in a civil society to allow people to make serious attempts to incite violence. The problem is not in this principle, but in the way it's being utterly misapplied to my situation. If the attacker had actually listened to and understood my sermon, he would not have assaulted anyone. Have *you* listened to my sermon, or have you formed your opinion based on what others have said?"

"Of course I've listened to it! And what you said was obviously hate speech. I have a quote right here." Ms. Hessen replied as she flipped quickly through her notes. When she found the quote, she began to read it to the pastor, "The Love Without Limits lifestyle is immoral. I *condemn* the LWL lifestyle!" Then she flipped her notebook shut with an air of finality. "That's hate speech."

"You haven't even quoted a *full* sentence. Please let me read to you from my sermon so you can get the context for those words." The pastor grabbed a piece of paper next to him and read,

I have searched the Scriptures. I have searched
my conscience. I've done my best to listen to and

understand the objections of those who disagree with me. And I've come to the honest conclusion that the Love Without Limits lifestyle is almost certainly immoral. And while *I condemn the LWL lifestyle* today as a sin, I am mindful of how God treated me and the rest of mankind in spite of our sinfulness. "All have sinned and fall short of the glory of God," Paul tells us in Romans 3:23[34]. God is all good and all holy. He hates sin. But although He hates sin, He surely loves the sinner. How do I know? "He demonstrated His own love for us in this: while we were still sinners, Christ died for us."[35] If I'm truly going to call myself a follower of Christ, I must love my neighbor, including my LWL neighbor. Therefore, I boldly stand before you today to call us all, including the LWLs no different than the rest of society, to repentance and offer complete and total forgiveness in the name of our Lord and Savior, Jesus Christ. Amen.

"How can this be hate speech?" he continued, setting the paper down. "To proclaim love for another is hate speech?"

"If Christians are supposed to love, then why are there Christians that run around committing hate crimes, like the man who listened to your sermon and then assaulted that innocent man?"

"We don't know if the attacker is really a Christian any more than we know what's in his heart."

"He went to your church! He calls himself a Christian! Don't try to disavow him now."

"Wait a minute. Just going to church doesn't make you a Christian any more than standing in your garage makes you a car.[36] So don't give in to the temptation to condemn Christianity based on the acts of those who claim to be Christian but fail to live by its precepts. The truth is, the Christian ideal has not been tried and found wanting; it has been found difficult and left untried."[37]

Back and forth the two went for several more minutes. Ms.

Hessen was becoming more and more irritated, as one does when one holds a certain point of view strongly but lacks the words or reasons to properly defend their view. Scrooge knew the signs well; he'd seen them often enough in his own debate opponents. Finally, she stopped listening altogether and was ready to end the conversation, making sure she had the last word.

"I think it's outrageous that you actually claim to love LWLs. You spin your point of view with a lot of hot air, but I don't buy it. It's thinly veiled LWL-phobia. And you're dead wrong about the LWL lifestyle being immoral and now an innocent man has been assaulted because of the intolerance you embolden under the guise of religion. But why should you care? All you care about is your precious right to ... hate speech. Furthermore, you underestimate the strength of the LWL rights movement. You should have considered the consequences to your family and church before you broke the law." As Ms. Hessen rose to leave, she concluded crossly, "When we get done with you, you won't know what hit you!"

In a sharp contrast to the incensed ranting of Ms. Hessen, the pastor looked quite despondent and spoke in almost a whisper, struggling to get the words out, "I do love the LWL. That young man that was assaulted ... is my nephew whom I love." But Ms. Hessen, who had been talking over him, did not hear his words and was gone a moment later.

The ghost looked at Scrooge disapprovingly but said nothing for the time being.

Although Ms. Hessen had seemed deaf to Bob's arguments, Scrooge had gained great respect for the pastor, who had not only delivered his point of view in a clear and logical manner but had done so with a coolness and graciousness that endured despite the hardship he and his family faced.

Scrooge was clear on Bob's central point, that it was logically inconsistent and unjust to take away the freedom of speech from one group in the name of tolerance toward another. Earlier Scrooge had ignored the fact that the law violated the very principle it was supposed to advance because the law worked to his advantage by stifling the church he sought to destroy. Now he was beginning to care. He thought to himself, *Although the law is specific in its application to those who opposed the LWLs, the principle it is based on can't exist in a vacuum. It could and would be applied to other situations. If it were legal to stifle moral free speech in one instance, why not another and another? Either the law will collapse under the weight of its corrupt precepts, or it be will be replaced by the rule of tyranny.* Scrooge was now sure that the bill was ill conceived, short sighted, and utterly dangerous to a free society.

"We can't preserve a free and civil society by enacting laws that empower the Thought Police[38] to silence those who disagree with us," Scrooge concluded aloud, as if he was informing the ghost of something he didn't already know. "Spirit, will this man be separated from his family and be forced to grow old in a prison cell for what appears to be the mere following of his conscience?"

The ghost did not answer.

"Spirit! Say he and his family will be spared."

"If these shadows remain unaltered by the future, no others of my race," replied the ghost, "will find him here. What then?[39] For you, just one less obstacle to a world free from religion. Where, oh Scrooge, does that sense of justice come from? And why should you listen to it? If God is dead, then all things are permissible.[40] How can we ground your moral sense of outrage with no transcendent moral lawgiver and no transcendent moral law enforcer? In your worldview there is no room for objective good or evil. What was it your father told you when he left home? Those are the breaks, kiddo."

Scrooge said nothing. The ghost seized Scrooge's hand, and they were gone again.

***

When they had finished their travel, they came to rest in the living room of a private residence that Scrooge did not recognize. But then came the sound of a hearty laugh, which Scrooge did recognize. Then came its owner – Scrooge's nephew, Fred.

"Ha, ha!" laughed Fred. "Ha, ha, ha!"

If you should happen, by any unlikely chance, to know a man

more blessed in a laugh than Scrooge's nephew, all I can say is, I should like to know him, too. Introduce him to me, and I'll cultivate his acquaintance at once. It is a fair adjustment of things that although there is infection in disease and sorrow, there is nothing in the world so irresistibly contagious as laughter and good humor. When Scrooge's nephew laughed so heartily – rolling his head and twisting his face into the most extravagant contortions – Scrooge's niece by marriage laughed as earnestly as he. And their assembled friends, not being out of step, roared out enthusiastically.

Scrooge could see it was now the evening of Christmas Day and he was now at Fred's party, the party he promised he would *not* attend.

"He said that Christmas was a humbug, as I live!" cried Scrooge's nephew. "He believed it, too! He's a comical old fellow, that's the truth."

"Shame on him, Fred!" said Fred's wife indignantly. "I have no patience with him." All the other ladies expressed the same opinion.

"Oh, I have!" said Fred. "I'm sorry for him. He takes it into his head to dislike us, and he won't come to dinner with us. What's the consequence? The consequence is that he loses some pleasant moments, which could do him no harm. I mean to give him the same chance every year, whether he likes it or not, for I pity him."[41]

Fred's sister-in-law interrupted, "Why pity him, Fred? After all, I've heard him say with his own lips that if he could work his will, he'd outlaw public prayer and organized religion all together. What justification has he to do such a thing?" When no one answered, she continued, "I'm not the most religious person, not nearly as much as you, but that idea could win a prize for being the most truly terrible. After all, wasn't it the Christians who built many of the first hospitals, schools, and orphanages? And this would be just the tip of the philanthropic iceberg when you consider the work that's being done today. Plus, Christian institutions have produced some of the greatest artists, musicians, and scholars of Western civilization.[42] How could anyone claim that all religion is bad and worthy of being outlawed in the face of the facts?"

Overhearing the conversation, Topper entered the room, walking carefully with a very full glass of wine in hand. He added facetiously, "Such a terribly dangerous thing – public prayer, huh? Perhaps it's not imminently dangerous, but you can never be too careful. Tomorrow the prayerful masses may be declaring jihad, so best just to throw them in jail today if they so much as say 'God bless you' when you sneeze!"

Topper spoke with such animation that he forgot that just a moment ago he was trying not to spill his drink. Now half of it was upon his sleeve and on the floor.

"Right," agreed Fred facetiously with a laugh, grabbing a paper towel and handing it to Topper to mop up the spill. As Topper quickly completed the job, Fred continued, "But I just can't help thinking there's good in him, that there's hope for him. I intend to persevere in an effort to find out if I'm right about him. He may rail against religion until he dies, but he can't help thinking better of it – I defy him – if he finds me going there, in good temper, year after year, and saying, 'Uncle Scrooge, how are you?'" After a short pause, he continued in a furtive tone, "I think I shook him yesterday."

It was their turn to laugh now at the notion of him shaking Scrooge. Fred, being thoroughly good-natured, and not much caring what they laughed at, just as long as they laughed, encouraged them in their merriment.[43]

The conversation drifted from Scrooge and after a while they played a game of trivia; for it is good to be children sometimes, and never better than at Christmas, when its mighty Founder was a child Himself.[44]

Scrooge's niece made herself comfortable with a large chair and a footstool, in a snug corner, where the ghost and Scrooge were close behind her. There might have been twenty people there, young and old, but they all played, and so did Scrooge. Wholly forgetting the interest he had in what was going on and that his voice made no sound in their ears, he sometimes came out with his guess quite loud, and very often guessed quite right, too.

The ghost was greatly pleased to find him in this mood and looked upon him with such favor that he begged like a boy to be allowed to stay until the guests departed. But this, the spirit said, could not be done.[45]

"Here is something new," said Scrooge. "One half hour, spirit, only one!"[46]

When the group had quieted down, Scrooge's nephew inquired, "Does anyone have a joke to share?"

"I do!" exclaimed Topper and leapt to his feet. "Here goes. Why did the toilet paper roll down the hill?" As witnessed during his performance at Sunday School, he was notoriously unable to resist embarrassing himself whenever he felt there was a good laugh to be had by doing so.

"I don't know. Why *did* the toilet paper roll down the hill?" replied Fred, trying to be a good sport in spite of the childishness of Topper's joke.

Standing up, Topper exclaimed, "To get to the *bottom*!" And as he said this, he pointed to his own hindquarters in order to leave nothing to the imagination. This rather close knit group of guests fell victim to the urge to laugh – perhaps laughing because the joke was so bad, not because it was so good.

Scrooge, who was not impressed by Topper, turned to the ghost and sarcastically queried, "Not afraid to stampede across the line from clever, self-deprecating humor to buffoonery, is he?"

Other guests, now emboldened by the thought that their jokes couldn't be any worse than Topper's, shared their jokes with the party – all receiving approval and laughter. Last to go, Fred exclaimed, "Oh, have you ever heard the joke about the four men on an airplane?"

No one had.

"Well, there were four men on an airplane – the pilot, a mountain climber, a pastor, and a professor.[47] The pilot came out of the cockpit and announced to the other three men, 'Gentlemen, both engines have failed and we're going to crash. There are four of us and only three parachutes. This is my plane, and the parachutes are mine, so I get one of them.' Before anyone had time to disagree, the pilot with the parachute already on this back jumped to safety.

"The professor then stood up and spoke. 'I'm Dr. Ebenezer Scrooge,' said he, 'a world famous atheist professor! The world needs me because of my brilliant intellect – I must teach the ignorant masses about the truth of atheism – I must survive!' Without waiting for the other two to agree, Dr. Scrooge grabbed a parachute and jumped.

"Now the mountain climber and the pastor were left facing each other with a single parachute between them. The pastor spoke first." Here, Fred spoke the part of the pastor dramatically, as if retelling some epic tale, rather than telling a joke. "'You take the last parachute, my friend. In the name of Jesus Christ, I will die so that you can live.'

"The mountain climber was silent for a moment, perhaps unable to comprehend the benevolent gesture of the pastor, but then he replied, 'Um, that won't be necessary. You see, the *brilliant* atheist professor just jumped out of the plane with my backpack. There are still two parachutes.'"

With that, the guests burst into laughter and some even applauded as they considered the idea of Scrooge becoming a human pancake somewhere far below the troubled airplane.

"He has given us plenty of amusement tonight for sure," said Fred, "and it would be ungrateful not to drink to his health. Here is a glass of mulled wine ready to our hand at the moment; and I say, 'Uncle Scrooge!'"

"Uncle Scrooge!" they cried.

"A Merry Christmas and a Happy New Year to the old man!" said Scrooge's nephew. "He wouldn't take it from me, but may he have it, nevertheless. Uncle Scrooge!"

The whole scene passed off in the breath of the last word spoken by his nephew; and Scrooge and the spirit were again upon their travels.[48]

***

Scrooge was not angry at the joke, but he was humbled and embarrassed. He called out to the ghost in the darkness of their travels, "Spirit?"

"Yes, Scrooge?"

"Did you think that joke was funny?"

"Ha-ha! Oh, I believe it was clever, blithe, and most demonstrably funny!"

"I get it, you know. An arrogant man's selfish plans backfire and he learns the hard way the high price of pride. I've always been able to take a joke," Scrooge announced, conveniently overlooking the recent incident in the pub where he had expressed his wish to punch each of the three older gentlemen in the pub in the nose after they delivered a barrage of jokes about his prideful behavior.

The ghost let Scrooge's boast pass and focused on the heart of the matter by saying, "In truth, one's presuppositions are a lot like what one grabs before jumping out of an airplane. If you get the backpack instead of the parachute and have already jumped, it doesn't matter at that point how smart you are. In truth, you have no proof for naturalism in all of your learning; it is merely a presupposition – something you assumed at the onset. "No miracles allowed" is merely a handy mantra you could shout while jumping from the proverbial airplane.

The ghost next dealt with the morality implied by the atheistic worldview as highlighted by the joke.

"If one lives true to an atheistic view of the world, then a 'me first' attitude is rational. According to atheism, you humans are merely organisms trying to get your DNA into the next generation. Dying for a stranger makes no sense. 'Me first' is a more honest response, although it makes one uncomfortable and does not make for good small talk at a party. No, an atheist can't be too honest with others, or perhaps even with himself, about this inconvenient, little truth."

Scrooge was not buying it. "Pardon me, but as an atheist, I can know right from wrong, and even more – I can choose to do the right. I've always viewed Marley and many other atheists as friends who were pleasant and kind, and more so than many a crusty old religious sourpuss. Let me tell you, Spirit, a well-mannered atheist professor with a mastery of social niceties is sure to impress."

"But what's the source of those good manners? Is there any good reason to think that there's anything more than a 'social contract' form of morality at work, where the atheist is motivated to be nice simply because he gets ahead in society by playing by the rules? In other words, one fulfills his contract by doing what's in the common good and is rewarded by society. One can choose to be good enough to keep one's friends and stay out of jail, or one can chose to do more if there's an adequate reward for doing so."

"If it works, what's the problem?"

The ghost just stared silently at Scrooge. Just as the silence was beginning to make Scrooge uncomfortable, the ghost asked Scrooge a question. "What about when it's no longer in the atheist's best interest to be nice ... like when the group is short one parachute?" The ghost paused to let Scrooge recall the joke and continued. "The atheist has no good reason to be anything other than selfish. In that way, an atheist is 'morally free' to break any old contract and forge a new one whenever it becomes convenient or when the benefit of breaking the old contract is greater than the possible social cost. In fact, one is free to act as ruthless and treacherous as ..." The ghost pretended to struggle for an example.

"Hitler," said Scrooge sheepishly.

"Thank you! ... as treacherous as Hitler so long as one is powerful enough to avoid the social costs of doing so. I can summarize your social contract morality with one sentence – 'You scratch my back and I'll scratch yours.' What if the atheist dies "scratching another person's back" for instance by giving up the last parachute?"

"In that situation, death precludes the possibility of getting like treatment in return," Scrooge answered, conceding the obvious.

"If the atheist fails to think of himself first, good for him! But the fact remains he's simply not living in a manner consistent with his worldview. So when the chips are down, in what worldview is it logical to give your very life for another? Atheism? Surely not!"

Scrooge had no response for the ghost. In the past, the moral system that atheism implied had occasionally bothered him in vague ways, but he had managed to not think about it too deeply – until now. Whenever the problem threatened to rear its ugly head, Scrooge managed to confuse the issue in his own mind by focusing only on the specific instances where social contract morality worked well enough. But in light of this kind of "moral freedom," his worldview was ultimately morally bankrupt.

Although Scrooge could not see the ghost during this entire conversation, apparently the ghost had seen him and commented, "I can see that you're bothered deeply by where your thoughts have led you. Of all things, a joke has tied you in knots!" With that declaration the ghost again unleashed his dreaded laugh.

The ghost and Scrooge came to rest in an open field on the outskirts of town. It was dark except for the light of the moon. In the distance Scrooge could make out the glow in the sky from the city and more nearby the clock tower of a nearby building. While Scrooge remained unaltered in his outward form, the ghost had rapidly grown much older. Looking at the spirit as they stood together in an open field, Scrooge noticed that its hair was gray.

"Are spirits' lives so short?" asked Scrooge.

"My life upon this globe is very brief," replied the ghost. "It ends tonight."

"Tonight?"

"Tonight at midnight. Hark! The time is drawing near."

The chimes from the clock tower were ringing the three quarters past eleven at that moment.[49]

"Forgive me for asking," said Scrooge, looking intently at the spirit's robe, "but I see some strange flashes of light, harsh to the eye, escaping from your robe."

"Look here." The ghost spoke in a low, but angry voice. From the folds of its robe, it brought a mirror. Its reflections were so bright and clear, it surpassed what Scrooge could see with his own eyes unaided. "Oh, Man! Look here. Look, look, here!" exclaimed the ghost, pointing urgently toward the mirror. He continued as if each word pained him dearly, "Greater love has no one than this: to lay down one's life for one's friends.[50] But God demonstrates his own love for us in this: While we were still sinners, Christ died for us.[51] Love was God's plan for your life, and love was the example He set. The purpose of the mirror ...is to show you as you really are. Come, look closely if you dare!"

At that moment, the mirror's reflection hit Scrooge's face squarely for the first time. He looked briefly, then averted his eyes, appalled at the sight of his face in the mirror, grotesque as the picture of Dorian Grey.

The ghost continued now with more ease, as if sharing the image in the mirror with Scrooge somehow lifted a burden from it. "What was it that Jacob Marley's ghost told you earlier? 'You're in rebellion from God,' I think he suggested. Well, that image in the mirror might just be what rebellion from God looks like. And what was it that you told your nephew earlier? 'You believe a myth!' I think that was it. Apropos. Now tell me about your social contract morality that you've clung to all these years! How does it look in the mirror?" The ghost continued to hold the mirror to Scrooge's face and stared silently at Scrooge as his words sunk in.

Scrooge tried to say he looked delightful, but the words choked themselves, rather than be parties to a lie of such enormous magnitude. The sight was repulsive, beyond any analogy, but what made it more than merely ugly, but also truly horrifying, was that it was him, not because the ghost had said so, but because Scrooge could see it. This was his own face, not as it was that day, but scarred by every wicked thought and deed of a lifetime. Deeds long ago forgotten were fresh on his face as if they had just happened, there on display in the reflection of the mirror. "What if God exists?" Scrooge whispered. The possible implications were unspeakable.

The bell struck twelve. Scrooge looked up from the mirror

toward the clock tower while it chimed, then looked around him for the ghost and it had vanished. As the last stroke ceased to vibrate, he looked behind himself and beheld a solemn phantom, draped and hooded, coming, like a mist along the ground, towards him.[52]

Look and read, and brave the peril,
Sing to this new Christmas carol,
Prodigal wanderer, king of misgiving
What happens next is dying or living

STAVE IV – THE LAST OF THE SPIRITS

The phantom slowly, gravely, and silently approached. It was shrouded in a deep black garment, which concealed its head, its face, its form, and left nothing of it visible save one outstretched hand. Except for the hand, it would have been difficult to distinguish its figure from the night and separate it from the darkness which surrounded it. It was tall and stately, and its mysterious presence filled him with a solemn dread. When it came near him, Scrooge bent down upon his knee. The very air through which this spirit moved seemed to scatter gloom and mystery. He knew no more about it, though, for the spirit did not speak.

"I am in the presence of the Ghost of Christmas Yet To Come?" asked Scrooge.

The spirit did not answer, but pointed onward with its hand.

"I know this might be an act of great condescension on your part to even answer me, but are you about to show me shadows of the things that have not happened, but will happen?"

Again, the spirit did not answer, but pointed onward with its hand.

Although well used to ghostly company by this time, Scrooge

feared the silent shape so much that his legs trembled beneath him as he rose, and he found that he could hardly stand when he prepared to follow it. It thrilled Scrooge with a vague uncertain horror to know that behind the dusky shroud, there were ghostly eyes intently fixed upon him. Though he stretched his own to the utmost, he could see nothing but a bony spectral hand and one great heap of black.

"Ghost of the Future! I fear you more than any specter I have seen. But since I know your purpose is to do me good," Scrooge declared, though actually quite uncertain of the specter's purpose, "I am prepared to bear your company and do it with a thankful heart. Will you not speak to me?"

It gave him no reply. The hand was pointed straight before them into the pure darkness which soon covered them both.

**

The darkness then gave way to dim cloudy late afternoon light. They were in the back seat of a small car driven by Scrooge's nephew, Fred. Topper, sitting in the passenger seat, spoke, "Thanks again for having me over last week. I always enjoy hanging out with your family."

Fred smiled. "When you are going to get yourself one of those, eh?"

"What? A wife and family?" Topper sighed heavily, the sadness of it shocking coming from one Scrooge had witnessed acting so silly. "It should have happened long ago. The problem is, my Sunday school routine isn't the only thing that's a comedy of errors – my life goes that way too. Did I ever tell you what happened to me a few years ago?"

"I don't think so."

"Senior year, I met this girl named Lori in one of my classes. We had been dating for a couple of months, and I really thought she was something special, thought… well, maybe hoping she was the one, although it was really too soon to propose. Well, around Spring Break that year, my family and I went on a vacation to the beach and I brought a couple of buddies. Lori planned to be there too with her girlfriends and we met up at the beach on a Saturday. It was early afternoon when I found a place that rented bikes nearby. Well, they had tandem bikes! I had never ridden one before and decided it would be too much fun not to give it a try. So, I convinced Lori to go with me on a tandem bicycle. I also convinced my buddy, Lawrence, to come too. He rented a regular bike and was riding solo along with us. We were having a great time – at least I was. But apparently my riding was a little too adventurous for Lori. I was going too fast and taking too many chances with the way I drove the bike. She normally enjoyed my horsing around, but got really annoyed with me this time and wanted to get off. Ultimately we decided the best solution was for Lori and Lawrence to change places, so Lawrence began to ride the tandem bike with me and Lori rode solo on the bike next to us.

"Well, believe it or not, some of the Spring Breakers at the beach mistook Lawrence and me for a couple. It started out with them calling us names and telling us to get off the beach. I was shocked. I mean, I know Spring Break isn't known for good behavior, especially on a beach where there's a lot of drinking going on, but these people were really mean. We all knew it was a case of mistaken identity. Even so, their comments were very unkind and struck me as very wrong."

"Yes, that sounds like a very bad scene," Fred agreed as he continued to drive the car.

"That's for sure. It didn't end there, though. On an ill-advised second pass by the Spring Breakers, they started to chase us and throw things at us, all the while calling us the worst names you can imagine. We managed to escape from the beach area quickly, but not before Lori got hit by a rock meant for me and Lawrence. It cut her leg. She was OK, didn't even need stitches, but it was all very disturbing and very scary for all of us."

"So did things not work out with you and Lori?"

Topper looked down at his hands. "Well, … she didn't blame me for the way we got treated at the beach, but things went downhill pretty quickly anyway."

"But she took a rock for you. She sounds like a good sport."

"Yeah, but... Lawrence was pre-med and offered to look at her leg after the ride. Lori accepted the offer. I could tell by the way they interacted then that it was gonna be trouble for me. Not only was Lawrence smart, he was also one of the university's top tennis players ..."

"Uh-oh."

"Yup. And he was frankly just a whole lot better looking than me. It's like I just disappeared to them after that bike trip. I wanted to say, 'Hey, Lawrence, you know that's my girlfriend you're flirting with?' and to Lori, 'Hey, you're my girlfriend. You're supposed to laugh at *my* jokes and look at *me* that way, not him!' But it would have just been too pathetic and frankly pointless. Topper was out and Lawrence was in."

"That's brutal. It would have been hard for you to compete with Lawrence in the categories that seemed to be most important to Lori, but he didn't have your quality of character, that's for sure. Too bad ol' Lori didn't put a premium on that."

Topper shrugged. "He was supposed to be my friend and he moved in on my girl. I'm sure Lawrence is a great guy – in ways that I'm not aware of."

"Well, if I know women like I think I do, I'm sure you caught the eye of a half dozen or more of the single ladies teaching Sunday School with your amazing performance last week. The way you interact with kids is priceless. You're marriage material for sure, my friend."

Topper finally looked up and managed a wan smile. "Thanks, buddy."

They had pulled into the parking lot of the church, but between the car and the church entrance was a group of LWL protestors. Scrooge noticed some had signs; some were waving at cars as they passed on the street; some were in costumes, and all were protesting the church and its notorious pastor. Fred and Topper parked the car and started to approach the building, but a large group of about two dozen protesters attempted to block their path.

"Don't go into this church," someone shouted. "Don't have

anything to do with it. The pastor here is a hate-filled bigot. He has no love for LWLs! Don't align yourself with an anti-choice hater."

Judging by the protestors' demeanor and words, Scrooge sensed they were not interested in a thoughtful give-and-take dialog. Their presence in front of the church was about intimidation, as were their angry words. Perhaps Fred sensed the same thing, since the normally outspoken man would not utter a word to this group or even look any of them in the eye. His face was grim as he kept what he thought was a safe distance and contemplated a strategy for getting by the blockade.

Topper was less discerning though, perhaps frustrated by having this confrontation so soon after reliving the memory of the Spring Breakers. Regardless of the reason, Topper declared to the protestors, "The last time I checked this was still a free country. Freedom of assembly and all that! Besides, people don't get things done with angry lynch mobs anymore. That's so last century. Get with the times."

"The skinny one thinks he's funny," shouted a voice from the crowd. "If the LWLs aren't free, ain't nobody free! Someone needs to teach this ignorant bigot to keep his mouth shut!"

Scrooge wondered what freedom the protestor thought the LWLs were lacking... perhaps the "freedom" to force everyone to agree with his strongly held beliefs. The LWLs already had the right to practice their lifestyle without interference. What had caused the pastor and the church to run afoul of the LWLs was the withholding of approval of and the voicing of concerns about that lifestyle. As ugly as the crowd's mood was, though, Scrooge wondered whether it was even safe for Fred and Topper to proceed or whether they should just go back to the car.

His question was answered only a second later. Before Fred could even turn around to appeal for calm, a rock landed square against Topper's forehead with a thud. To Scrooge's horror, Topper's knees buckled as his eyes rolled back in his head. Fred lunged ungracefully to grab Topper as he fell and did manage to save him from crashing to the pavement. While the crowd screamed obscenities, Fred scurried to get a better grip on Topper, lifted him swiftly over his shoulders in a fireman's carry, and like a Marine bearing a wounded buddy out of battle, began sprinting across the parking lot, making his way back to the car and away from the mob. By the time the two reached the car, Fred was gasping for breath and a stream of blood from Topper's forehead was making a steady drip onto the parking lot. Fred wrenched open the front passenger door and eased his unconscious friend into the seat, then slammed the door shut again and turned to put up a defense.

But the protestors didn't follow Fred and Topper back to their car or give them any additional trouble. They were too distracted by the brigade of police cars that had just pulled into the parking lot. Scrooge couldn't imagine how the police had arrived so quickly or who would have made the call.

As the squad cars drove past Fred's car, he tried in vain to wave them down to alert them to what had just happened and to get help for Topper. Scrooge joined in the waving, forgetting that he was seeing but a shadow. Strangely, though, the police cars ignored Fred's signaling and rushed to the front entrance of the church. Once the officers had parked their cars, they proceeded directly into the church. Apparently, they were at the church for another reason.

Looking forlorn, Fred dragged himself to the driver's side and got in the car. Then he looked over at Topper, who was still out cold, and asked, "Well, buddy, shall we stick around to see what the police are up to, or should we get you to a hospital?" With that, Fred pulled out of the church parking lot and drove away.

Scrooge could not help see the irony of this violent scene. Earlier, Topper had had rocks and bottles thrown at him by a group of students on Spring Break who'd mistaken him for an LWL. Now the LWLs had mistaken him for the moral equivalent of those Spring Breakers, and he'd had rocks thrown at him again. He was under fire from both extremes and hadn't deserved it from either side. "This poor boy just can't win," Scrooge concluded empathetically. Then in the midst of all the confusion, the scene before Scrooge and the ghost faded away.

***

When they re-emerged into the light, the ghost conducted him through several streets until they entered the Cratchit's apartment and found Emily and two of her children seated round the kitchen table. Conspicuously missing were the father and the oldest son. Emily was clearly distracted and worried. Martha was reading, but Tim was rubbing at his leg and looking pained.

"Mom, my leg hurts again," declared Tim.

"It's growing pains, son," his mother replied absently.

"I'm hungry."

"Supper won't be long now. It must be near your father's time to come home," Emily said to both children.

"He's actually pretty late," Martha answered, closing her book.

"Your father loves the church very much and staying late is no trouble, no trouble. He has a soft heart for doing his service for the church."

Martha agreed and they were very quiet again.[53]

Someone approached the front door, but the fact that whoever it was knocked dashed Emily's hope that it would be her husband or son. She rose to answer the door and found the caller to be the woman who normally taught the three-year-olds in Sunday School.

The woman at the door looked grim and didn't bother with greetings. "It's happened as we knew it most certainly would." Then she caught sight of the children and said no more.

Emily excused herself to the children and stepped out into the hall of the apartment complex, closing the door behind her so that they could speak freely. "They've... they've taken Bob?"

The other woman nodded. "They've taken him into custody, charging him with violating the hate speech law. They came to the church this afternoon while I was working in the office."

"When can I see him?"

The visitor could only shake her head and shrug.

Emily had to know what was almost certainly in store for her husband and her family. He would be far away in a federal prison, and the children would grow up without their father. As if she had already been separated from him for a lifetime, she gave a wordless cry of grief and began to weep.

The woman from the church hugged her for a moment but then backed away, holding her firmly by the shoulders. "Emily, I know it hurts. Lord, how I know it hurts. But you've got to be strong for the kids – and for Bob. You have no choice."

Emily tried to stem the flow of tears and then agreed. "I know. I know. The children won't be able to deal with this without the love and guidance of their mother."

Although Scrooge would admit nothing to the specter, he got a chill, then a sinking feeling as he realized that this pitiful scene had been caused by him. He had really managed to hurt this woman and her innocent children – a devastating hurt.

Emily invited the woman inside and called the children to join them by the Christmas tree. Once they were all settled, Emily took a deep breath and, praying the children could understand, began, "Your father loves each of you dearly, but he can't come home for a while." Over the buzz of "Why? Why?" from the children she further explained, "Well, honestly, your father is … um, in trouble with the police."

"Why doesn't Dad just do what the p'lice want?" Tim asked. "Then maybe they'll be nice and let him come home."

"Dad would love nothing more than to do that, honey, but what they want him to do is wrong. Oh, how he dreaded the possibility of this day coming. Even though it's not easy, he's doing what his conscience tells him is right – and that's a good thing. God in his sovereign plan sometimes calls us to do difficult things and even make sacrifices for the things we know are right. That is what Dad is doing, and that's why he can't come home for a while. God will watch over Dad and us. Everything will be fine." She choked back tears with her last sentence, which made it sound less than convincing. "We'll pray for God to help this be over soon, and we'll trust Him to work all this for the good."

"Your father has a lot of support from good people who will fight on his side – many in our own congregation," added the woman from the church. "Take the kindness of Mr. Fred. After Sunday School last week, Fred sought out Pastor Bob, saw that the pastor looked just a little down, and inquired what had happened to distress him. Being the most pleasant-spoken gentleman you ever heard, he said, 'I am heartily sorry for your trouble. If I can be of service to you in any way, here's my cell. Please reach out to me.' Now, it wasn't the thought of anything he might be able to do for your father or the church, so much as Fred's kind way, that made this so touching to Pastor Bob. It really seemed as if Fred felt for him."[54]

"I'm sure he's a good soul!" Emily agreed. "As is your father," she added as she turned back to the children. "But however long we are apart from him, I am sure we shall not lose hope or goodwill."

"Never, mother!" the children cried.

"I am very happy," said Tim courageously, "and I'm proud of my dad!"

Emily kissed each of her children and hugged them tight.

The Ghost of Christmas Yet To Come raised his arm, and darkness fell on Scrooge.

***

The light from the family room window then reappeared, but neither the ghost nor Scrooge moved. Through the window, Scrooge could see the street outside the Cratchits' front window, and as he watched he noticed a slow change in the seasons from winter to spring, then summer, fall, and winter again. Suddenly the room came into full view again, with Emily and the other woman now seated on the couch. Emily was gasping and sobbing, her eyes hollow and raw with emotion. He found it very difficult to listen to and even harder to observe. His mind raced at what could have possibly gone so wrong to evoke such raw emotion.

"It will be OK," the other woman said, almost pleading. "Please don't lose hope."

Scrooge wondered if Emily's deteriorating spirit could be

attributed to her husband's having been in prison for the year he'd just seen pass.

When Emily was able to speak, she spoke softly, and the tears didn't abate. "You… you don't understand. My Tim is sick, very sick."

"What's the matter with him? Is it serious?"

"It's cancer."

The other woman gulped but tried to stay positive. "There's a lot they can do for cancer, right? There's a chance he'll be OK. What did the doctors say?"

Emily could barely whisper as she shook her head. "It's at Stage IV."

The friend was still a bit confused. "How many stages are there?"

"Only four. It's metastasized and inoperable. The cancer is everywhere by now. He had been complaining of knee pain on and off since last Christmas. But we initially assumed it was growing pains, and then with all the uproar over Bob's arrest, and … by the time I was finally able to get him tested, it was too late. It's untreatable. I'm going to lose my baby boy!" she sobbed loudly.

"Oh," the other woman whispered, as if the breath had been knocked out of her lungs. "I… I didn't know. I'm so sorry."

Scrooge frowned fiercely as Emily struggled to pull herself together. "That's … just wrong. He's an innocent boy. And this is too much for this mother to bear …"

He could have continued, but he stopped himself as the words of the Ghost of Christmas Present ran through his mind again. "Where, oh Scrooge, does that sense of justice come from? And why should you listen to it? If God is dead, then all things are permissible."[55]

What happened next surprised Scrooge greatly. The other woman spoke, , "We do not worry like those who have no hope.[56] We believe Jesus died and rose again, and through Him we'll triumph over every trouble in this life – conquering even death itself."

Emily raised her head, took a deep breath, and smiled through her tears. Scrooge could hardly believe it. Emily, the Christian, was still listening to talk of real hope at a time like this. Scrooge stood quiet for a moment thinking to himself, then spoke. "What hope could I, as an atheist, offer the mother of a dying child? I could explain the facts according to atheism: We live and we die ... and that's it. If you suffer or have a bad life, then what's your consolation?" Scrooge thought for a moment then continued, "There is none – those are the breaks, kiddo."

Those are the breaks, kiddo. Scrooge contemplated those words from his father as he reflected on the day his father left him and the day his mother died. He knew the hollow ring of those words all too well.

"But where is the comfort? Where is the hope?" Scrooge asked looking up at the spirit. "Is there any to be had, Spirit?"

The ghost gave no reply, but instead raised his arm and brought on the darkness that accompanied each change of scene.

***

In an instant they were no longer in the city, but instead deep in the country, but Scrooge did not recognize the countryside. He saw uninterrupted, rolling white hills of snow that sparkled in the sunlight. It was winter, it was quiet, and it was terribly lonely, notwithstanding the company of the taciturn ghost which was like having no company at all. There were no sounds, as if the birds had either fled or were too afraid to sing. The air was so clear and dry that Scrooge thought he might be able to see forever across the seemingly endless succession of hills. They walked along a path for a very long time. The path upon which they walked was covered in snow and had short wooden fences on both sides covered in a thin coat of ice that gleamed in the sun. After what seemed to Scrooge like a very long and lonely time of walking, the phantom stopped and directed Scrooge to depart from the path, cross the fence in a space where the rotted fence beams had fallen in disrepair, and to continue up a great rolling hill through the snow to the top where one lone tree stood. The tree was also covered with a coat of ice and the branches sparkled like tinsel.

Scrooge obeyed the specter and proceeded to the top of the great hill.

At the top behind the tree, Scrooge discovered the young man he had met by the cemetery before his adventure began. The boy looked much older now, five to ten years older, Scrooge guessed. His head was down and his manner solemn. He wore a fierce expression and to Scrooge's eyes looked quite distraught. As Scrooge approached he could hear the young man having a strange conversation with no one in particular. He sounded lifeless as he muttered, "Always winter, always gray, always dusk, never day. This season I'll celebrate reason." Scrooge looked around and saw that there was no one else present. The young man had been talking to himself. Scrooge wondered what dark train of thoughts had led him to such a depressed state of mind.

"What's to celebrate though?" the young man continued. "Timmy's dead. Scrooge is dead. Heck, even God's dead!" He pulled a piece of paper out of his pocket that was crumpled and looked as if it had been torn from a book, then read aloud with a sudden burst of energy. "God is dead and we have killed him! How shall we, murderers of all murderers, comfort ourselves? That which was the holiest and the mightiest of all that the world has yet possessed has bled to death under our knives. Who will wipe this blood off us?"[57] He then put the paper down and continued with a frantic lecture in his own words, "The death of God brings with it the inescapable death of purpose, the death of moral values, and … our own death. It follows rationally according to the second law of thermodynamics; entropy will lead to the eventual heat death of the universe. All life will cease and all of our gain erased to nil. This is not science fiction; this is real science.[58] The conclusion is inescapable! We are nature's accident. The earth is our death row holding cell. We are all going to die soon; we're all going to die alone; and we're all going to stay dead.[59] There is no hope. There is no escape. There is only the insufferable agony of awaiting our fate. Any other conclusion is intellectual laziness. Therefore, I say again," repeating his mantra, "it is always winter!"

There was something sickening about this nihilistic speech, something that struck a pain deep within Scrooge's heart. He wanted to offer some comfort to this man who was clearly mad with despair, but what could he say? Scrooge thought aloud, "In an atheistic worldview, this young man is dead right. If natural processes continue unimpeded, all things will decay, and as entropy increases, the universe's temperature will eventually approach absolute zero. All our efforts will be reversed to zero. The hope for mankind is zero."

While Scrooge found himself agreeing with the logic, he felt there was something quite wrong, though he couldn't quite name it. One thing was certain to Scrooge, though: the young man he had met on the street had definitely grown up in this thinking since their original meeting.

Then Scrooge noticed a rope with a noose at the end of it lying at the foot of the tree. "Heavens!" he cried in shock. "Is he going to hang himself?"

There was no reply from the specter. The young man rose, picked up the rope, and threw the end of the rope with the noose over the first branch of the tree.

"I feel responsible in part," continued Scrooge. "I set him on this path. I need to counsel him. I cannot have his blood on my hands!"

The ghost only pointed at Scrooge, then pointed back to the path. Scrooge momentarily defied the command of the specter and grabbed frantically for the rope as the young man secured the other end to the trunk of the tree, but seeing his hand pass through the rope again and again, Scrooge only reaffirmed that he could have no impact on what he saw. The man and the rope were only shadows of the future.

So he turned to the ghost and pleaded, "Please, tell me that I might return to my life that I might intervene in some way and change this shadow."

The ghost did not reply. He only pointed at Scrooge, then pointed back to the path. Scrooge stood frozen in his tracks for a moment in defiance of the ghost, but without a chance to intervene in some way, Scrooge knew his protest was pointless and acquiesced to the command of the ghost. They left the despairing young man behind on the hill as their march through the countryside continued. The light in the sky grew less and less and the horizon they faced glowed in pink and orange. As they walked on and on for what seemed to Scrooge to be many hours, each hill became greater than the next.

But he couldn't get the young man's words out of his mind. "Is life without God truly meaningless?" he asked aloud. "Is it absurd? Just a day ago life seemed so full and worthwhile to me, but when I consider honestly how it all ends, how every last thing that gives me happiness and comfort in this life is stripped away, one by one, like the leaves of a tree in the fall, it all seems like a terrible, cruel joke. And as I reconsider my life, those very days when life seemed to abound I now find to be merely an earlier stage of a purposeless race toward non-existence." Scrooge did not like where his thoughts were taking him. He shook his head. "There has to be a loophole. I must be missing something."

As he walked on, he went over the arguments again and again like a broken record until he was absolutely mentally exhausted. Even so, he would resist the urge to doubt his atheism. As much as his emotion and intellect were beginning to fail him – there was something stronger yet that he could fall back on. He thought of it as "resolve." Scrooge said to himself, "My intellect will not fail. This fight will not be over until I say it's over, and I have not given up yet." And he began to whistle defiantly, ignoring the shrill, desperate edge to the tone as it echoed through the desolate, otherwise silent hills.

Finally, there was a distraction – a structure of almost incomprehensible size began to emerge in the distance as they came over the crest of a mighty hill. It was a large gothic sort of building, not unlike a cathedral or castle, but much larger than anything he'd ever seen built by human hands. It stretched on and on, far into the distance. Its top was intermeshed with the clouds that glowed with the colors of the dying light, and its walls faded away to the horizon, becoming one with the sunset. As beautiful as the building was, it looked ominous and uninviting, like a sleeping giant against the evening sky.

The specter led Scrooge down the long and snowy path toward this building and through the large front doors, which Scrooge guessed were at least five stories tall. The doors were open as if expecting them and led into a large hall. As soon as they were inside, the doors closed behind them with a resounding slam – perhaps by the will of the phantom or by some will of their own. Once closed, the doors and the entire back wall of the hall disappeared into the darkness. Inside, it was dimly lit at best and absolutely silent. Scrooge caught a faint smell of candles, torches, or something of that sort and tried to identify the source of the dim light but could not. Beyond a hundred feet or so, everything in the building was lost in the darkness, giving the building the sense of having no beginning and no end. Scrooge could make out a musty, dusty smell that he usually associated with old buildings which in the darkness and the stillness made him feel the weight of ages in the air.

The walls on the left and right were near enough so that they were only slightly visible as dark shadows. The specter led Scrooge over to the walls to get a better look. Lining the wood paneled walls on both sides Scrooge could see giant painted portraits; each picture was many times larger than life size. Scrooge recognized many of the faces, some of them famous and some not so famous. But all the people he recognized had two things in common: they were all atheists, and they were all dead. Why they should be here, Scrooge could not know. And why Scrooge himself was here, he could not know, either, since the phantom would not or could not speak.

Scrooge wandered further down the hall with the phantom flanking him as he went, and the dim light seemed to travel with them. They continued around one bend and then another until far ahead he could see the hall open up into a great room where the lighting was more substantial. In that great room there was a marble lectern at the top of a long, winding marble staircase. Both the stairs and the lectern shone a bright white. The light that illuminated them was like a spotlight, but Scrooge could not find its source. Beyond the lectern, the room again disappeared into the darkness. As Scrooge and the ghost drew closer, Scrooge could see a book resting on the lectern.

At the spirit's prompting, Scrooge approached the staircase, passing the many faces in the portraits on both sides of him. Each face in the portraits seemed to stare at him. Although he might have expected it, he was taken quite off guard when he spotted the portrait of his old friend, Marley. His face in this picture seemed lifeless and sad -- sadder than Scrooge had known him in his earthly life or in his ghostly visit earlier that evening.

Scrooge could relate to the expression on the face of Marley's portrait. He wished his friend could speak to him again; the room was cold and lonely, mysterious and unnerving, and he just longed for someone to tell him things were going to be OK. But he received no such assurance. And as he passed Marley's portrait, it suddenly occurred to him that the portraits might be of those that had come here before him. The thought only increased his dread.

Across the remaining distance of the great room and up the stairs the specter led Scrooge. The staircase was built against the left wall, upon which Marley's portrait hung, but after several stories the staircase bridged across the room to join the right wall and continued its ascent several more stories. This pattern of bridging from wall to wall continued until the staircase reached the top, which was at a dizzying height. Each stair's height and depth was several times that of a normal stair, which caused Scrooge to consider climbing them with his hands and knees, but he was just able to throw his leg high enough to take the steps in an upright stepping fashion so long as he held to the railing with his hand for balance. Normally this would have been an exhausting climb for Scrooge, but in his current state of existence, while his emotional and mental anguish were real, he hadn't the faintest notion of fatigue and physical discomfort. But given the prior scenes with the Ghost of Christmas Future, the emotional and mental stress alone were nearly overwhelming.

Ultimately, he and the phantom reached the top, stepping onto the lofty rostrum and approaching the lectern holding the book. It was a very large book indeed. Like everything in the building, it seemed larger than life. The book's cover was extremely ornate, made of gold and silver and decorated with jewels. The precious metals were melded into intricate patterns and designs, but they only acted as a frame of sorts to the pictures that dominated the cover.

The pictures on the cover were whimsical and childish in nature -- bunnies and teddy bears, flowers and a sun, all with smiley faces. The pictures were done in bright primary colors that one would expect to find in a kindergarten classroom, so that when taken on the whole, it kind of looked like a giant book of nursery rhymes for the toddler children of some giant king.

Next Scrooge read the inscription on the cover of the book. It was a poem.

Look and read, and brave the peril,
Sing to this new Christmas carol,
Prodigal wanderer, king of misgiving,
What happens next is dying or living.

Scrooge guffawed in relief. "This *is* a giant nursery rhyme book!" he cried. Every other experience thus far with the Ghost of Christmas Future had been quite overwhelming, and his nerves were raw. He tried to shout a very forced, "Bah! Humbug!" in the hope that it would make him feel more like his old self again, but he gave such a weak delivery that it only served as proof of how shaken by the whole experience he was.

Scrooge considered the message in the poems and was too smart to ignore the reference to peril, but felt that perhaps the very reason he had been brought to this place was to read the book. For what reason he should be egged on by a poem, he did not know. He felt he had nothing to lose and could think of no reason why reading a book might be dangerous, especially a giant nursery rhyme book, so he opened it.

On the first page of the book it was mostly blank white with a few words written in Latin in the center. It read, "Audenter Dicere, Veritas Legere."

Scrooge knew just enough Latin to know that it could be translated something like, "Speak boldly. Read the truth." He decided to ask the big question that was on his mind. "I'm tired and frustrated – being confronted with the question of God's existence now by a host of ghostly ambassadors of theism, not to mention my ridiculous nephew, Fred, but isn't this really an impossible question to answer? What do you say to a person who argues that belief or disbelief in God is often times no more than a guess? Isn't the practical thing to do when time and resources are unavailable to simply remain a skeptic or indifferent?"

At once the page began to fill with a written response.

Is belief in God ever a blind, wild guess?
You will see it is not, it's important to stress.
But let's now assume guessing is all one may do
Is skepticism the most rationale view?

So let us weigh up all the gain and the loss.
If it's true God exists and if He is your boss,
Then if you choose yes and to Him bend the knee
What do you gain? You gain eternity.

But if there's no God, then what here do you miss?
Maybe some passing and counterfeit bliss.
Or maybe you find you lose nothing but strife
If godly living yields a more blessed life.

Now what of the atheist's side of the bet?
If God exists and you're wrong, you'll have naught but regret.
You may gain fleeting freedom and some passing pleasure,
But it costs you eternity, which lasts for forever.

And if you are right that God is not there,
You gain things of this world, but then die in despair.
So let's now review which belief should persist.

Do not hesitate. Wager that God exists.[60]

"This is like blackmail." snorted Scrooge indignantly, ignoring that he had asked the question of God in the context of guessing. "Believe in God or God might punish you for eternity. Nothing but theological bullying. Well, I won't be blackmailed. And furthermore, Marley suggested God was after my heart. Now this argument says nothing about a decision of the heart. It seems to argue for belief in God based on motivation for what's in one's own selfish self-interest. That strikes me as an odd way to approach the subject."

Although Scrooge did not admit anything, it *did* secretly appeal to his pragmatic side because it relied on game theory and represented a practical strategy for self -preservation that was free from sentiment.

He continued, "As interesting as this argument may be when considering belief, I'm unmoved. I'd rather make the bold claim and say, 'God is dead.'[61] Let someone prove me wrong!" When he had finished this statement he looked back at the page to notice that new writing was beginning to appear.

Now defend your view in whole.

Lose this fight, lose your soul.

Scrooge was not expecting this confrontational tone in reply. This place was eerie and a bit overpowering, and a book which produced its own script was nothing short of mysterious. He had spoken the words "God is dead" to be provocative, nothing more. Although he meant what he said, he was not actually looking for a fight. But now he was in one, apparently.

"Lose my soul? How can I lose what I don't have?" said Scrooge flippantly.

The writing continued.

Why does there exist something at all

When nothingness seems more logical?

If there were no Maker to be the cause,

Our mere existence should give us pause.

"How can any man know why something exists instead of nothing? I don't know. No one knows."

The writing on the page continued to appear as the book continued the debate.

If Leibniz's premises[62] go through,
The claim, God exists, is most certainly true:

Premise 1: Everything that exists has an explanation of its existence, either in the necessity of its own nature or in an external cause.
Premise 2: If the universe has an explanation of its existence, that explanation is God.
Premise 3: The universe exists.
Conclusion: Therefore the explanation of the existence of the universe is God.

Now pick here a premise that you reject
Or the existence of God is what you expect.

Scrooge smiled and mumbled in contempt, "So, we're going to debate the question of God's existence." He understood the game he was playing and he knew there were two ways to win: show that the premises of the argument did not actually imply the conclusion by using the laws of logic, or demonstrate that at least one of the premises was false. If he could do either, it would invalidate the argument and avoid the conclusion. The stakes were high, though; if the argument's premises were all true and it had a logically valid structure, then the conclusion must be true as well. He quickly reread the syllogism, examining the structure of the argument against the rules of logic to assess whether the conclusion logically followed from the premises:

"If it is true that the universe exists and that everything that exists has an explanation as premises 3 and 1 claim, then I must conclude that the universe has an explanation.

"If it is true that the only explanation for the universe is God as premise 2 claims and if it is also true that the universe has an explanation as is implied by premises 1 and 3, then it follows that the explanation of the existence of the universe is God, just as Leibniz claims."

Already, one of the two means of winning the game was closed to Scrooge. The argument did have a logically valid structure.

Strangely, in all of his years of railing against the existence of God he had not encountered Leibniz. Scrooge thought to himself, "Leibniz must be some crank theologian.[63] Once I have a chance to consider each premise carefully, I will rise to the challenge and find the flawed premise, and retire this silly syllogism to the scrap-heap of theology."

Scrooge assumed his opponent would hide his flawed assumption at the end so he started with premise 3, but was quickly disappointed.

"Premise 3: The universe exists." Scrooge read, paused for a moment, making a few faces of feigned deep thought. "Shall I disagree? Can I disagree? On what grounds? OK, mysterious book, I'll grant that premise 3 is true. The universe does exist."

Immediately the word "Correct" appeared on the page next to the premise.

"So onto premise 2: If the universe has an explanation of its existence, that explanation is God." Scrooge paused to think, this time with a focused expression. The pause only lasted a moment as his sharp intellect drove itself to a firm conclusion. "Well, now, I expect that you expect me to reject this premise. You probably assume that I'd reject any premise that posits God as a possible explanation for anything, but I'm smarter than the average atheist, so we won't have to waste a lot of time arguing this point." He got a confident, but sinister grin on his face and continued, "I don't reject God as the explanation for the universe *if* the universe has an explanation. The real problem for the theist is that the universe *does not* have an explanation. The trick hidden in this premise is that it is the logical equivalent of another statement that I and virtually all atheists accept, namely that if God does not exist, then the universe has no explanation. And as a result, though I reject Leibniz's conclusion, I accept that this premise is true."

Immediately the word "Correct" appeared next to the

premise.

"So your trick must be waiting for me in premise 1." Scrooge was a little concerned to have conceded two of the three premises so quickly, but he was still confident in his ability to see through this argument and show it as false. He read slowly, "Premise 1: Everything that exists has an explanation of its existence, either in the necessity of its own nature or in an external cause." His face wrinkled with disapproval. "Sure. Things that exist have an explanation. Babies exist and the explanation of their existence is that their parents conceived them. Automobiles exist and their explanation is that they were made in an assembly plant. But if *everything* that exists has an explanation and I supposed for a moment that God exists, then what, mysterious book, is the explanation for God?"

Without delay an answer began to appear on the pages of the book.

Do you not know the definition of God?
Or do you ask as some type of facade?
The uncaused Causer, eternal Creator,
The unmoved Mover, the world's Initiator.
If God exists, you must certainly see
That He exists by necessity.

Scrooge reread premise 1, "'Everything that exists has an explanation of its existence, either in the necessity of its own nature or in an external cause.' So according to this premise, if God exists, His existence would be explained by a necessity of His own nature. I guess God cannot by definition, as the greatest and most powerful being, have an external cause or that external cause would be God.

"But what if the present state of things is explained by an infinite regress of explanations? You don't need God if every effect has a corresponding cause and this continues backward into an infinite regress of explanations." Scrooge was quite happy with this mind-bender.

He didn't have to wait long for a reply, as the book's writing began again at once.

Consider the argument as here defined.
This world's present state is not all that's in mind.
Include rather all the things past that are done.
Lump all time and all space together as one.

All matter and energy are included here too.
This is what's meant to be within your purview.
Define that as the universe and ask again 'Why?'
The infinite explanations don't explain the whole pie.

But each explanation only explains each little piece,
And man's curiosity still hasn't decreased.
One explanation for all *things is needed*
And only one here in the end will be heeded.

So even a multiverse or a universe everlasting
Needs an ultimate explanation or there's no sense in asking.[64]

"So you're telling me that when Leibniz refers to the universe he includes *all* time, *all* space, *all* matter and *all* energy. Thus, the only explanation you leave for the universe is something that transcends the universe – some necessary being that transcends all time, space, matter and energy. I guess that brings us back to premise 2, 'If the universe has an explanation of its existence, that explanation is God.' I've already conceded that, so I seem to have run into a dead end there. But even though positing an infinite regress of explanations is not helpful to refuting this argument given the way this argument is worded, I can still part ways with Leibniz and say this premise is *false* and therefore conclude that the conclusion God exists is *false*. As I mentioned a moment ago, the universe simply exists *without* explanation! The most reasonable belief is that we came from nothing!" Scrooge announced triumphantly.

To his surprise, though, rather than admitting defeat, the book continued the debate. He tilted his head and raised his eyebrows as he reluctantly read again.

Believing you came here from nothing is tragic.

It's far worse than saying you believe in magic!
What reason have I for a statement like that?
At least the rabbit has the magician and hat! [65]

But to pop into being from nothing, "ka-pow!"
Will have every magician asking you, "How?"

Scrooge was caught off guard by this accusation. Weren't the miracle-loving Christians the ones clinging to fairy tales and magic tricks? How dare this book accuse him of believing in something *worse* than magic! But what could he say in reply? He had just finished insisting the most reasonable answer was that the universe came from nothing.

The writing in the book continued, seemingly intent on doing more damage to Scrooge's claim that the universe exists without explanation.

Read here this story. [66] *Perhaps you might see*
Why explanations are necessary:

Two scientists walked in the woods in the fall
And spied there a pumpkin-sized, translucent ball.
The first scientist said, 'Whatever could be
The cause of that thing of such great mystery?'

The second scientist replied abruptly to him,
'There's no sense in asking! You're really quite dim!
In truth, that odd object exists unexplained,
And its reason for being's forever unnamed!'

Should the first scientist just accept this reply,
Abandon his question, and bid it good-bye?
Well, the first scientist just pulled back his fist
And then let it go toward the second scientist.

The result was much pain, a cracked nose and black eye.
The second man clutched at his face and he cried,
'What explanation have you for assaulting me!?'

But the first shrugged and calmly said, 'Why make that plea?

'The punch that I threw, well, it's just unexplained,
And its reason for being's forever unnamed.'
Now scientist 2 saw the point of the first scientist:
We should expect explanations for things that exist.

Now scientist 2 was a staunch atheist
And scientist 1 had a thought and couldn't resist.
Since now he had gotten his foot in the door,
He decided to ask just a few questions more.

'What if the ball was a wee bit more grand?
Would the need for an explanation still stand?
Not the size it is now, but the size of a horse?'
Scientist 2 replied, 'Don't be silly, of course.

'Size isn't the critical fact in the case.
The ball could be as big as… as all outer space,
And the need for an explanation would stand.
Consistent reasoners will make that demand!'

'Well, now,' said the first man, 'and this is my point
In putting your poor nose just now out of joint,
Good scientists know explanations are key.
To claim none is needed is quite contrary

'To doing good science and thinking that's fit.
To expect explanations but suddenly quit
When the object's a universe-size of a ball
And its explanation is God or nothing at all

'Is to treat explanations like just so much trash.
It isn't good science; it's really quite rash.
To claim that the universe is unexplained
And its reason for being's forever unnamed

'When everything else has an explanation behind it
And the whole point of science is to go out and find it[67]
Is just an escape from what's abundantly clear -
The existence of God is all that you fear!'

Stunned, Scrooge stepped back from the lectern but tripped and fell to the floor of the rostrum. He knew that the joke was on him. How could he, as an honest scientist and clear thinking person, demand and seek explanations for everything else but then dismiss the need for an explanation when the explanation for the universe was in question? It was arbitrary. Even more, it was a thinly veiled attempt to avoid the conclusion that God in fact exists. He knew the only explanation of the universe was something that transcended the universe. He knew there were theories of multiverses and that a multiverse could offer a possible explanation of this universe, but that only succeeded in pushing the question back one step. It created a new question: What is the explanation of the multiverse? He needed an ultimate explanation that terminated the series of intermediate explanations that only a universe-transcending, necessary being could provide.

He thought for a moment what his options were at this point, and then he stood up, approached the lectern again, and spoke. "I don't know for certain if premise 1 is true, but I strongly suspect that everything that exists probably has an explanation for its existence."

Immediately, the word "Correct" appeared in the book.

Scrooge was emotionally shaken. He realized what he had done. He had admitted all three premises were more likely true than false. He knew the syllogism was logically sound and that true premises implied a true conclusion. In a nutshell, he had been given a good reason to doubt his atheism. He stepped back from the lectern again, this time careful not to trip. The thought that God might actually exist repulsed him. The further thought that God, somewhere, somehow, might be behind this whole nightmare enraged him.

"Why is God putting me through this? Why doesn't God just

leave me alone?" he muttered. He thought of his father, then of his mother. The pain of those memories through the visit of the Ghost of Christmas Past had become more intense than ever. Then suddenly with all the outrage he could muster, he shouted into the darkness, "If God exists and is all powerful, then why is he letting all the misery in the world take place? Why doesn't he just end it now and get it over with? WHAT'S HE WAITING FOR?"

Scrooge's voice echoed against the mighty walls. The book did not write this time. Oh, how he wanted the book to write for him. Whatever it wrote he planned to rip it out and tear it to shreds. There was a long silence where nothing happened. Finally, a loud and piercing voice responded from behind Scrooge, out of the darkness – the voice of his old friend, Jacob Marley. "HE'S WAITING FOR YOU, SCROOGE!" Marley shouted back. "THE REASON HE HASN'T ENDED IT IS THAT HE'S WAITING FOR YOU!"

Scrooge was ready for a good many answers from the book, but not an answer so personal from a friend who knew him. He could have accepted any answer other than that. God was waiting for him? Marley had said earlier that God was after his heart and that it was actually Scrooge who was running away. Scrooge had insisted that if it were reasonable to believe in God, he would. Now the truth was on display. When given a good reason to believe in God, he was repulsed.

Marley's voice continued, "He's kept you and this world around all these years because He's waiting for you and the rest of His fallen creation to turn to Him. The One who created you and all of humanity is waiting for you to come home."

Scrooge was not about to show the impact Marley's words had just had. He protested further, "Why assume God loves me? Why not assume He hates me, or perhaps He's just indifferent? Why turn to God and serve Him as you suggest?"

There was silence.

After waiting a moment, Scrooge returned to the lectern. "Please, mysterious book, write. I will listen, but please *just* give me answers." His eyes were glossy with tears of frustration, but he spotted that more writing had begun in the book. He read the pointed message aloud,

Why serve God? Why not just serve your needs?
First of all, He made you. You belong to Him,[68] indeed.
Human nature proclaims now that you're your own boss,
But if there's one thing that you must avoid at all costs,

It's trusting your nature – it's fallen and misled.
But if nature's no guide, where should you turn instead?
God shows us Himself in a few important ways:
He's revealed in His creation where the universe displays

His limitless power and ability to confound us,
Which shows His ways are greater than our own or those around us
But also man's heart is marked by transcendent design.
We're signed with a conscience that's from the divine.

It's a sign of His goodness, a sign He is just.
And there's more, as if these signs alone weren't enough.
He's revealed Himself in Scripture you remember from your youth.
Explore it to know His love, explore it to know the truth.

Scrooge took a deep breath and gave a disappointed frown as he exhaled slowly. "Now I'm being confronted with the Bible? I've been a good sport, haven't I? I've listened to this crazy, rhyming diatribe. I've been nice and given my thoughtful critique. I really would be much obliged not to be confronted with the Bible, OK? After all, isn't the Bible just the wishful thinking of humanity? So what if there's a God? Why chalk up the Bible's message of heaven as anything other than wish fulfillment by human beings?"

The mysterious book responded with more writing.

If the Bible were mere wishful thinking by man,
Then 'heaven for all' is the message it'd send.
A grand compromise where sin's pleasure's OK.
Want to be selfish? God just looks away.

Not the demands for perfection before a holy, just King,
Not the laws and the judgment that His justice will bring.
Not repentance for sin, embarrassed and weak
But partners with God where we get to speak

Of what rules apply and what's right and what's wrong.
History's rife with men singing this song.
The inconvenient truth we can't face so it seems
Is our fall from God's grace and His work to redeem.

Like a hammer and anvil the true Word is spoken,
And man's wishful thinking is fatally broken.

"So if the Bible tells us we're in big trouble with our Maker, this would not exactly qualify as wish fulfillment... not anything *I've* wished for, anyway. In summary, then, God made us, He loves us, but He hates our selfishness and His justice demands a sacrifice? I suppose this is where Jesus comes in and saves us?" Scrooge asked somewhat flippantly. He was badly rattled, but could still cling to one point of skepticism. "Please! I've really been more than a good sport. Don't confront me with Jesus though. Do you really think you can turn me into a 'Jesus freak?' Why should I accept that Jesus was really God? Why can't we just assume he was a great moral teacher or something?"

Marley's voice arose again from the darkness. It rang out in the hall with a distant echo, "This man, Jesus, claimed to be the God of the universe. If that claim is not true, then He was either a lunatic or a liar, and therefore hardly a great moral teacher. If His claim is true, then He is the God of the universe and infinitely more than just a great moral teacher."[69]

"Marley, my friend, are you telling me you somehow became a follower of Christ?" Scrooge asked into the darkness. When there was no reply he continued, "What about hell? Can anyone tell me what business does a loving God have sending people to hell anyway?"

Scrooge hoped he would again hear Marley's voice, but this

time the book answered.

What are you hoping that God will do?
Give all those on the highway to hell a redo,
Pay for all of their crimes, no matter the cost?
He has done this already – he paid on the cross.
If not forgive them, then what choices remain?
To get out of their life, freedom from Him obtain?
Then they are free from His peace if the truth here I tell.
But this peace-less "freedom" has a name … it is hell.

Suddenly, Scrooge recalled the words of the old man in the pub when he was with the Ghost of Christmas Past. "I fear that God will not force him into heaven against his will. And it seems to me that this boy's pride has him racing down a road that leads far away from God. …"

Scrooge pondered those words for a moment, then continued, "… And leads to hell, itself? Marley said all a person has to do to avoid hell is to stop running from God, but how can you know for sure what will satisfy God? How can you know something as elusive as the very will of God?" His tone continued to convey tiredness and frustration, but had now changed in a very distinctive way – no longer sarcastic or flippant, but sincere. Scrooge waited for an answer, but to his great disappointment he received none.

While he had many unanswered questions, both the rhyming book and Marley's Ghost had led Scrooge to a most remarkable place. He was now asking questions with an open mind – not seeking to reinforce his doubt, but seeking to know the truth if he could. He was to the point of considering with an open mind the *possible* truth of the ideas he'd been confronted with: that God exists, that we need to be reconciled to Him because of our moral crimes, and that God has promised redemption through Christ's death and resurrection.

Scrooge then pondered quietly. "Perhaps there's no certainty to be had by anyone – the believer or the unbeliever, but if God really exists and is both perfectly loving and perfectly just …" Scrooge paused a moment to weigh his next statement and then continued, "This just might make at least *some* sense.

"None of my alternatives seem good anymore. It's probable that God exists, but not certain. I believe that everything needs an explanation which includes the universe and the explanation of the universe must be something that transcends the universe. A being that transcends the universe is the common sense definition of God.

"Furthermore, when I think of the evil in the world, the evil in humankind's heart, I think there must be an objective Good to be the standard to give the word 'evil' meaning at all. I believe in objective good and bad, but what are those words without an objective Law Giver and an objective Law Enforcer to ground them and to make them meaningful?

"And what is the meaning and purpose of life in a world without God? Did the young man with the hangman's noose have the answer, or is there lasting value in human existence after all – real value that only a transcendent source could provide?

The Christian explanation probably offers a valid answer to these questions and a valid explanation for why the world and mankind are the way they are.

"But … what about miracles? Could I ever become a crazy miracle-lover like Fred? Could *I* believe in the possibility of miracles? I'd become a laughingstock." After a long pause, he reconsidered the words of his nephew. "What was it that Fred said? 'If God exists and created the universe, then any other miracle you imagine is too difficult for God is in fact a piece of cake compared to the creation of the universe out of nothing. This would include raising Jesus from the dead.' Am I really justified in ruling out miracles anymore?

"And lastly, there's my reflection in the mirror to consider. Courtesy of the Ghost of Christmas Present, I saw my own face somehow scarred by my every wicked thought and deed. The reflection was more hideous than the portrait of Dorian Gray. If I'm to get to heaven on my virtue, I'm not to get in at all. How can I know for certain that even I could somehow still avoid my perdition? Please, book, … Jacob, … someone, answer me."

The book wrote one last sentence. "It's your time." And then, in a sudden, swift move, the book slammed shut. The light on the book went dark.

Scrooge was startled and cried out, "No! Wait! I have more questions. I'm not ready yet."

But he would not receive additional time to question the book. Being reminded that there was some pre-ordained agenda that he had no control over and that might be entering its final moments, he became a nervous wreck. He wasn't sure what was in store for him next. What did that last sentence, "It's your time." mean? Was he about to commence his own march down death row?

Soon Scrooge regained his composure just enough to begin to consider his options. He wanted nothing more than to run from the specter. He looked at the specter who was standing very near him silently with an outstretched arm, pointing down the staircase. But if he ran, where could he run to? He was still trapped between life and death. There was nowhere he could run that was out of the specter's reach. He forced himself away from the lectern and reluctantly began the walk down the oversized stairs and down the hall, with the specter leading the way.

As he walked past the portraits again, he noticed something he somehow hadn't noticed earlier. Above each portrait, somewhat out of sight unless one happened to gaze upward and look carefully, was an engraved plate. But the plate didn't contain the name of the deceased, as Scrooge would have expected. Instead, the inscriptions were titles like "The Kalam Cosmological Argument"[70] or "The Argument from the Fine-Tuning of the Universe."[71] Many portraits had the same inscription, but there was still a good variety. Scrooge read the plates as he walked by: "The Argument from the Origin of Information in the First Living Organisms,"[72] "The Moral Argument,"[73] "The Argument from Irreducible Complexity in Biology,"[74] "The Transcendental Argument,"[75] "The Argument from True Miracles including the Resurrection of Jesus of Nazareth,"[76] "The Argument from Human Desire,"[77] and so on. In total, there were more than two dozen or so different inscriptions, all apparently arguments for the existence of God.[78]

The thought occurred to Scrooge that such a grand place must be very special to God. Scrooge imagined this hall could very well be a trophy room of sorts for God of all the atheists the book had triumphed over. Now, the nature of the triumph was unclear to Scrooge. Had the book merely defeated them by winning a debate like the one Scrooge had just participated in? If so, what then? Had God left them to face their perdition, or was there something else accomplished?

The specter stopped and raised his hand pointing at a blank space on the wall. Scrooge had been so lost in thought that he had not noticed that they had reached the area where Marley's portrait hung. The specter stood in front of an open space next to Marley's portrait. Then in a slow, deliberate manner the specter produced a new portrait from his cloak and placed it on the blank space on the wall. Scrooge felt he knew whose face he would see. While it gave him a sickening thrill to even think of it, he could not resist the morbid urge to look.

The new portrait was his own, and the plate above the portrait read "Leibnizian Cosmological Argument."[79]

"No... no, Spirit, take this portrait away!" Scrooge, cried, feeling that his time of judgment might be near. He asked the most important question he could think of: "Why have I been taken through all this if I am past all hope!? Is there hope for me?"[80]

In asking the question, Scrooge was beyond intellectual curiosity at this point. He cared about nothing except the possibility that there might be hope. The specter did not answer, but suddenly the wall behind the portrait opened up to reveal a passageway. The specter pointed to the opening as if to beckon Scrooge to enter. Scrooge reluctantly edged his way through the threshold of the opening into a narrow hallway, perhaps with the tiniest shred of hope that it was the way home. It was dark in this hallway so after a few steps he stopped. As he stood there peering ahead, he was just able to see that within a few feet of where he stood there was no floor beyond, only a drop-off. He edged closer to get a better look beyond the precipice – but he saw only a steep drop-off into utter blackness, a pit that seemed to emanate terror and sadness. Scrooge imagined that it had no bottom and that anyone who fell in would fall forever, becoming more and more isolated and removed from any source of comfort or peace. If he had blindly followed the specter's direction, he would have surely fallen, perishing into the blackness. Scrooge had dreamt in night terrors as a young child about this sort of place. The thought that this sort of place actually existed made Scrooge weak in the knees and again sick to his stomach.

He struggled to control his terror and whispered sadly, "I'm going to die. This can't be. I'm not ready. No." He turned his head in the direction of the specter who, to Scrooge's horror, had already entered the hallway blocking any escape and was slowly, inexorably closing in behind him. Scrooge called out, "How can I know for certain that God exists? How can I know if the promises in the Bible are true? How can I know for certain what will happen to me when I proceed into this darkness? I'm confused and I'm scared. Speak comfort to me!"

The specter did not answer, but Marley's voice spoke in a whisper as if Marley were standing right next to him in the darkness, "You can't know. You can either believe or not believe."

Scrooge peered out into the darkness, longing to see Marley or any familiar thing that could provide him comfort, but like a dark smoke the blackness only churned before his straining eyes. He called out to Marley desperately into the darkness, "Please, Jacob, I need more time to figure all this out. Can I be granted at least a moment?"

Marley's voice spoke one last time, loudly, echoing in the darkness, "The thing that must be done does not take more moments!"

Scrooge looked back to see that the specter was almost upon him. There was no escape now. The specter would surely push him into the abyss.

Did Scrooge think he had met his end? Let there be no doubt

that he did. And in light of the excruciating pressure of the moment, what he did next was most noteworthy. There was no fighting or yelling or shaking his fist, no final speeches or jokes or rude gestures. He simply bowed his head and closed his eyes. One might interpret this act as a pathetic attempt to escape the reality of his situation or perhaps as a sign of resignation to his perdition, but perhaps he silently called out to God, or perhaps he made a desperate plea for help overcoming his doubt.

There was hardly a moment enough for any of those options. In the next instant, Scrooge felt the bony hand of the specter. It grabbed him and lifted him with great force. But it was not so much the grip of a hand that lifted Scrooge, but a mighty force that encircled and lifted the specter and Scrooge both. Scrooge, helpless to resist, went limp. He had lost all control and had seemingly run out of moments.

STAVE V – THE END OF IT

In the dark, early hours of Christmas Day, shortly after midnight, Peter returned home. The runaway son whistled jauntily as he walked down the sidewalk leading to his home with a book jammed under his arm, a bestseller by Dr. Scrooge that he had just borrowed from a friend. He planned to "spend Christmas with Scrooge" by reading this book while sequestering himself in his bedroom, away from the rest of the Cratchit family.

Through the front door, past the family room, and down the hall to his bedroom; he went. By the time he passed his parents' room and saw no one inside, he began to realize that the house was empty.

"Weird," he thought, "but all the better. No one to disturb me while I try to read." Closing the door, he made himself quite comfortable to do some reading, but in spite of his efforts to read, perhaps because it was the middle of the night, he could not keep his eyes open. He pulled out the business card he'd received earlier that evening from his famous new friend, used it as a bookmark, and fell asleep almost immediately with the book still resting on his chest.

***

Meanwhile on the other side of town, Emily had found Scrooge's house and weighed the risks of disturbing those inside at this late hour. She hardly worried about offending Scrooge. As far as she was concerned, he was the most offensive person on the planet, but she didn't look forward to a possible confrontation of any sort. *What if Peter isn't there? What if he was joking? What if I misunderstood him somehow?* she thought to herself.

She texted Peter again but got no reply.

So what if Peter isn't there? That's precisely what knocking on the door will help me find out. She proceeded up the stairs that led to Scrooge's front door, the same stairs Scrooge had struggled up only hours before. She approached the door and the infamous knocker which, not looking anything like Marley's face, could not have looked more ordinary now. She rang the doorbell, which sounded more like a loud buzzer, and waited. She noticed some movement, then a women's face through an upstairs window, but the person to finally come to the door was a man dressed like a butler. He opened the door a crack and said, "What is the meaning of this? It's past midnight and Dr. Scrooge made no mention of expecting a guest."

"I apologize," Emily replied, "but I'm looking for my son. Do you know if Dr. Scrooge might have seen my son at any point this evening?"

"I don't know if he has or not. I'm sorry. I will leave him a note which he'll see in the morning. Will that do?"

"Please try to understand a mother's plight. I'm very concerned for the safety of my boy. I simply can't wait if I can get an answer from Dr. Scrooge now. Is that his window up there?" she asked, pointing to the third story window where she had spotted a woman's face.

"It is in fact his room, ma'am."

"If so, someone is awake up there. It might be Dr. Scrooge. For the sake of a worried mother, would you please check to see?"

The butler sighed and invited her to step inside and wait in the foyer while he went to check on Dr. Scrooge upstairs. Emily's boots were snowy and her feet cold, so the warmth and comfort of

Scrooge's house were a welcome alternative to the darkness and cold outside. But a moment later, she was struck with the deeply troubling thought that this house and all its beauty had been built on book sales that heaped ridicule on religion and promoted the restriction of free religious expression. The man who was destroying her family and her freedoms was inside this opulent estate probably sleeping like a baby without a care in the world.

Her thoughts were interrupted by a loud, clear cry from the butler. "Help! Call an ambulance! Call 9-1-1!" This was followed by a string of euphemistic explicatives and mutterings, like gee willikers and jiminy crickets.

Emily dashed up the stairs in the direction of his voice. Once she found the butler, she could see she was in Scrooge's bedroom. She did not see Peter, nor did she see the woman whose face had been at the window. Instead, she saw Scrooge's body on the floor and the butler on the phone following his own advice – calling 9-1-1.

Emily's first thought was one of schadenfreude. Scrooge had been so cruel and arrogant for so many years, and now he was lying there totally helpless, possibly dead. Although this did nothing to solve her problems – her son was still missing and the law Scrooge had helped to enact was still the law of the land – the sudden turn of events seemed like poetic justice.

The butler turned to her. "Do you know CPR? Can you help until the ambulance arrives?"

She stood there blankly for a moment. She imagined herself saying, *Oh, I'm really intruding. It's so late and I must get back to looking for my son. Good luck to you and Dr. Scrooge*, and then making a quick exit.

Yet the next thing she knew, almost against her will, she dropped down to the floor next to Scrooge. *From close up the man looks terrifying, almost like a troll*, she thought to herself. As she began to administer CPR, tears began pouring down her face. She hated this man. She wanted him dead. Why had God put her in this position of having to show mercy to her worst enemy? Yet somehow, she continued to administer CPR for 20 minutes, until the ambulance arrived.

No, Scrooge did not die, not on this day anyhow. Perhaps Emily would have found it some consolation in the moment to be reminded that he would in fact die someday. But on this day, on account of her efforts, he was revived.

***

Bob had driven the spider web pattern of DC streets for almost three quarters of an hour, getting more and more tired. One wrong turn can easily turn into two or three more in this city. Both children slept as he drove. He had switched over to listening to podcasts once the children had fallen asleep, but he was now too tired to pay close attention to the dialog on the podcasts.

Suddenly, he found himself passing Dr. Scrooge's home. Parked on the road out front were Emily's car, an ambulance, and a police car. His heart raced as he pulled over and parked. A moment later, he spotted Emily in the doorway. When she spotted the family's minivan, she came running. He instinctively got out of the vehicle and the two embraced.

A great number of unpleasant possibilities raced through Bob's head. "Why is there an ambulance here?" he finally asked.

"It's for Dr. Scrooge. He's had some sort of medical emergency." Before Bob could ask, she added, "Peter's not here."

"What happened to Scrooge?"

"When I got here, the butler went to check if Scrooge was awake at my request so that I could find out if he'd seen Peter tonight. But the poor man discovered Scrooge near death, and it was pure chaos after that!" She then looked Bob in the eye to make sure he understood her next words, "Against *all* my first instincts, I tried to save Scrooge's life while we waited for the ambulance to arrive. I so deeply wanted to walk away. I just wanted him dead, but I did what I knew I was supposed to do – I tried to save his life. I'm afraid it means we're ruined." With this last admission, she began to cry again, and Bob held her until she was ready to continue. "I did tell the police officer when he arrived that Peter was missing," she said then. "We've done all we can do tonight, I think."

"Seems so. Let's go home?"

She agreed and followed him home, exhausted and eager for sleep. Already it was sure to be the most sleep-deprived Christmas in years. Once home she led the way down the hallway, holding the hand of a half asleep Martha. Bob followed behind, carrying a sleeping Tim and turning off houselights with his elbow along the way.

Once Martha was in bed, Emily saw that Peter's bedroom light was on and poked her head in the door. There she found Peter at last, sound asleep in his room with Scrooge's book resting on his chest still. Relief mixed with exasperation washed over her, and her hand clenched on the doorframe. *Does he have any idea how much disruption he's caused this family?* she thought. *Does he know how much I worried and what I just went through?* She wanted to wake him up both to give him a piece of her mind, not to mention interrogating him about where he went.

But Bob, after finding her and sighing at the sight of Peter's oblivious face, put a gentle hand on her shoulder and nodded toward the master bedroom. Emily sighed in turn and nodded back, deciding sleep was the best thing for everyone at this late hour. There would be plenty of time to talk after church.

***

Everyone was very quiet the next morning, still worn from the chaos of the late night. The whole family, including Peter, rose and got ready for church. Bob rose first and was out the door first to get to the church in time for his Christmas Day pastoral duties. The others got ready a little later, not needing to be at church until just before the first service started. When Emily and Peter met in the kitchen they gave each other a nervous look. "Good morning Peter. Merry Christmas," she said in a subdued tone.

After a pause, he replied quietly, "Good morning, ... um, merry Christmas."

She was in no hurry to fall into another emotional argument with her son, and it seemed he didn't want any trouble from her, either. While she was relieved her son was still being cooperative about attending church, she was pretty sure his heart wasn't in it. She guessed he was just playing along since it was less trouble than fighting. The thought made her miserable.

When everyone was ready, the family piled into the minivan and started the short drive to the church. Emily and Peter's subdued approach to one another created an unfestive mood in the van when otherwise, in light of it being Christmas Day, it might have been the most joyous day of the year. Only Tim could break the gloom – and break it he did.

"Uh, Mommy, did we save Christmas last night?" he asked in a concerned tone as they drove along.

"I'm sorry, Timmy. What do you mean, save Christmas?" Emily asked.

"I mean, did we help Santa get all his presents back in the sleigh? Daddy said that you and Peter were helping Santa."

Emily smiled but was unsure what to say, especially since Peter was frowning in total confusion.

But Martha jumped to her rescue. "Yup. Dad found Mom and Peter with Santa just after you fell asleep. We put all the presents back in the sleigh. Santa was so thankful. I think I even saw a present with your name on it!"

Tim beamed a smile at his sister, but Peter slumped back in his seat, clearly trying to cover his confusion with insolence. Emily cracked a relieved smile.

After church, Peter went back to his room alone and made another attempt at reading the book by Scrooge. But the attempt would be short-lived. Bob came into the room a few minutes later and sat down on the bed next to his son. "Peter," he began, "do you know who Dr. Ebenezer Scrooge is and what he's doing to your family?"

Peter looked up nervously and shook his head. "No. I mean, I met him for, like, five minutes yesterday, and my friends always quote him. What's that got to do with us?"

"Scrooge isn't just your average celebrity skeptic. He has been working for a long time to rid the world of religious expression by any means – in particular the recent legislation that prohibits otherwise free speech that condemns the lifestyle of the LWLs."

"Yeah? So?"

"That legislation is designed to silence free speech and punish those involved, including those who are only following their conscience or the teachings of their religion. Your mom and I have shielded you kids from the troubling realities that potentially lie ahead for our family, but in your case, we're long overdue to give you a dose of reality."

"I still don't get it. What troubling realities? How does Scrooge's legislation affect us?"

"Someone who attended our church assaulted a member of the LWL movement after I called the LWL lifestyle a sin. So now I am in the crosshairs of this legislation. To be totally frank with you, if Scrooge has his way, I'll spend the best years of my remaining life in jail, separated from you and the rest of the family. This is very serious I'm afraid."

Peter's mouth hung open in shock.

"But that's not all you need to know, Peter. I don't know what happened between you and your mother yesterday, but when you weren't home by midnight, she was worried sick. I wish you could have seen her charge out of the house to find you. Her search led her to Scrooge's house, and as a result, Scrooge was discovered near death.

"What? Mom's trying to kill Scrooge?"

"Uh, no. Remarkably she did the opposite, son. No matter how much she might have wanted him to die, knowing what he's doing to our family, she worked to save his life until the ambulance came! If she can show that kind of love to such a terrible enemy, how much more must she love you, her own son?"

Peter shook his head, stunned. "I don't know what to say, Dad. But thank you for telling me what's actually going on. I had no idea, I swear."

Bob reached out to hug him, and Peter instinctively clung to his dad. It had been years since Peter had embraced his father that way.

"Come on," Bob said after a moment. "Let's go eat, OK?"

"Sure, Dad. Thanks."

After the family had lunch together, Bob left for what he hoped would be a brief meeting at the church with a reporter named Marissa Hessen. She had called him the night before requesting the meeting and shared that she'd already interviewed Dr. Scrooge. She urgently wanted to meet with him to discuss his views on the hate-speech law in time to include his side in an article whose deadline was fast approaching.

Peter and Martha were helping their mother clean up the kitchen after lunch when Peter said to Martha, "I'll handle clean up today if you want to chill."

Martha was dumbfounded. "Is this some kind of trick?"

"No. I'll do it myself today if you want. But it's a limited time offer, don't delay, act now," Peter said with a smile.

"That's the nicest thing you've ever done for me, I think. Why are you being so nice?"

"Ask me again, and I'll take back my offer."

Without any further questions Martha skipped out of the kitchen and off to her room.

Once Martha was gone, Peter turned to his mother. "Dad said you saved Dr. Scrooge's life last night. Is that right?"

"Yup." she replied with a smile.

"That's really amazing. I mean it's an amazing coincidence that you were there just at the right time and all, but I think it's even more amazing that you chose to save the life of someone that's done such lousy, rotten things. It's … . it's … um." Peter struggled for the right word. "It's good."

"You know why I was there in the first place, don't you, Peter?"

"You were looking for me?"

"That's right. I can't bear the thought of losing you to someone like Scrooge. I know you have doubts, Peter, and I don't fault you for that. But believe me, there are better answers to your doubts than the ones Scrooge is offering. Promise me you'll look for good answers."

"I thought you and Dad had all the answers."

"We don't, but perhaps we're content to live with a good number more mysteries in life than what's comfortable for you now. Dad and I will help you any way we can, but if we fail to give you the answers you need, realize that it's our failure and not the failure of Christianity as a whole. Just keep looking. God promised that if we seek for Him we'll find him when we search for Him with all our heart.[81] That's a great promise for any doubter to cling to, I imagine."

"Thanks, Mom. That sounds like good advice."

With that, Emily went to give her son the most heartfelt hug she could and ached with a combination of sorrow and joy.

"And by the way," Peter concluded, "I don't think you're weak-minded, not by a long shot."

Emily's smile brightened all the more.

When Peter finally went back to his room, he picked up Scrooge's book and dropped it in the trash. "Maybe it's time for me to start doubting my doubts," he said to no one in particular.

***

At the hospital, once Scrooge was stable, every test imaginable was run. Afterward, Scrooge slept much of Christmas Day but awoke when the doctor entered his hospital room. It was almost four o'clock in the afternoon. The bright sunshine from the morning was gone and the sun sank low behind gray clouds in the afternoon sky. Scrooge was drowsy, but felt good. The doctor quietly went about his work reviewing the test results. It was peaceful and quiet in the room, no Christmas excitement to disturb the patient's rest. The loudest noise was the occasional shuffling of papers by the doctor.

When the doctor was done with his review, he noticed Scrooge was awake. "Is it all right if I cover a few things with you now, Dr. Scrooge?"

"Yes. That's fine. Thank you, doctor," Scrooge replied.

"The test results are a bit of a mystery, but a good mystery. The aspirin in your bloodstream likely helped keep you alive until your lady friend arrived, and her fast action saved your life."

"What's so mysterious about my test results?"

"We know from the EMTs that your body temperature was very low when you were found and that your heart had been stopped for some time, possibly hours, depending on how long it took for you to be found. You were clinically dead, but your condition right now and the test results tell a very different story about your heart and your health. If I had only these test results to go by, then I'd have no real evidence you even had a heart attack. I don't mind telling you I'm quite perplexed. I was just asking one of the other doctors, 'Has ever a man recovered so quickly from such a horrid previous state?'"

In a moment of déjà vu, Scrooge recalled his own words the previous night, in which he prematurely declared his own recovery only to discover his corpse lying on the bedroom floor without him inside it. When Scrooge had first spoken the words, he thought his troubles were over, but they had just begun. Later, when he had lost all control in the hand of the specter and was past all hope of living, he had been delivered. Now hearing those words again, this time from the doctor, this time after a seemingly real recovery, Scrooge was struck by the irony. He couldn't believe what the doctor was saying.

"Are you quite sure, doctor? Am I really recovered?"

Scrooge half expected the doctor to yell no, turn into a ghost, and drag him into the next life. But instead the doctor just smiled. "You're as normal as any man your age, according to the tests. It's quite remarkable. You ought to be quite thankful."

"Oh, I assure you, I'm the most grateful man on earth today."

"You'll be released from the hospital and can recuperate at home. I'm sure you'll be glad not to be in a hospital the entire day on Christmas."

Scrooge smiled and thanked the doctor as the doctor made his way to the door. With that, Scrooge got dressed into his street clothes, called his butler, and checked out of the hospital. Minutes later the butler arrived with Scrooge's car and drove him home.

At home, Scrooge rested in bed, not so much because he needed it, but because he wanted time to think. He pondered the memories of the difficult evening just past. Could he believe that all the things he experienced were real? The doctor had said that the blood test showed that he had taken aspirin, which had helped to save him, and not a hallucinogenic drug as he suspected. Perhaps there was some other naturalistic explanation. But rather than indulge this line of thought further, Scrooge stopped himself. His reason wasn't that there was no possible naturalistic explanation. Perhaps there was, but as the Ghost of Christmas Past had suggested earlier, maybe that wasn't the relevant question to ask. Scrooge realized the better questions perhaps were whether the ideas and arguments that he had been shown during the past night were well reasoned and logical. Did they convey the truth?

Scrooge then spotted his housekeeper walking down the hallway out of the corner of his eye through his open bedroom door. The memory of seeing his housekeeper discover him "dead" but doing nothing to help him, even stealing from him, interrupted his thoughts. Scrooge got out of bed, checked the drawer, and found the cash was still missing. Since realizing that Scrooge would live, she must not have had a chance yet to return the money … or else she hadn't intended to. No one dreamt he would return from the hospital that same day. He promptly returned to his bed.

"Here, here," bellowed Scrooge into the intercom to anyone who could hear him. "I need to see my butler and my housekeeper at once."

The two promptly came in upon hearing their employer's voice. Both wore smiles as they entered the room. This politeness was their usual custom, but Scrooge had always assumed it was staged and that their smiles were phony. The butler's smile was extra toothy and wide. Scrooge imagined he was in quite a self-aggrandizing mood given his heroics from the night before.

"I wish to thank you both for saving my life," said Scrooge, pretending not to know that only the butler had done anything.

"Oh, you're welcome. I was happy to do it," said the butler promptly.

"Uh, you're welcome." said the housekeeper in a barely audible voice.

Scrooge continued, "Words are fine sometimes, but not in this case. No. I mean to thank you both in a tangible way. So do me a favor and go to my dresser. You probably don't know it, but I've been using the top drawer to store a good deal of cash. Please bring it to me. I wish to make a gift of it."

Scrooge imagined that this would make the housekeeper's heart pound a little faster. She knew the money wasn't there. The butler quickly began searching the top drawer of the dresser and soon all would know the money was missing. She slowly made her way to the dresser and pretended to help the butler search for the money.

As he searched, the butler asked Scrooge nonchalantly, "Dr. Scrooge, sir, did you know the woman who visited here late last night who helped to save your life?"

Scrooge pretended not to hear the question. "Look here, haven't you found that money yet?"

After a few moments of additional searching the butler announced, "The money seems to be missing."

"I agree," added the housekeeper quickly.

Scrooge feigned a concerned look and said, "Whatever could have happened to it?"

He wondered whether the housekeeper would come clean and beg for mercy or whether she would try to lie her way out of things. Thinking back to how cold and unfeeling he had been with her and to others in her presence, he guessed she'd view lying as the safest route.

"I don't know, Dr. Scrooge. Are you sure this is where you left it? Maybe you're mistaken?" she gently suggested.

Scrooge nodded his head with a feigned smile. Perhaps she thought he was agreeing with her, but as he nodded, he was actually was thinking, *Yep, I guessed right. She's lying.* He then blurted out sharply with a sudden change in disposition, "Please empty the contents of your pockets."

Her left pocket was, of course, where the money had been

stashed. Scrooge had seen her put it there. She paled and hesitated just a moment too long.

Scrooge yelled as best he could, "Please! Don't waste my time. Reach to the bottom of your pockets and show me what you have!"

"I'm so sorry. Please don't get too upset," she pleaded as she produced the money and handed it to Scrooge.

"Would you just let me get upset if I want to get upset?"

"I'm sorry! I meant to return the money."

"Come now! Would you believe an apology if you were in my shoes listening to it?"

"I don't know. Perhaps not, sir," the housekeeper replied meekly.

Scrooge glanced over at the butler, who had an amused smirk plastered on his face like a spectator at the Coliseum who had just seen the human contestant stumble in front of the lion. Perhaps he found the housekeeper's predicament amusing. "Perhaps she was just going to iron and starch those bills for you?" he offered.

"Uh-huh," muttered Scrooge not amused. He held a menacing expression on his face as he plotted his next diabolical step.

As if trying to read his boss's mind and fearing he had been too flippant a moment earlier, the butler blurted out, "Would you like me to call the authorities, Dr. Scrooge?"

Scrooge raised his eyebrows and pretended to consider the butler's suggestion, but did not speak. As the housekeeper's fate hung in the balance, Scrooge thought of the joke Fred had told at the Christmas party, the one about the parachutes. Scrooge clearly had the upper hand here; he was holding the parachute. He could let the housekeeper "crash and burn with the plane." It would be so easy, and she deserved it. She had shamelessly betrayed him and left him to die, and the amount of money she had stolen was not insignificant.

"You didn't help to save my life, did you? You saw me lying on the floor, didn't you?" Scrooge asked rhetorically and continued in a voice that slowly rose in both volume and fierceness, "Not only did you leave me for dead, but you stole from me as well. Now if I let the butler call the authorities as he's inclined to do, you'll be arrested, thrown in prison, and separated from your family for years. You're so old, you'll probably *die* in prison!" Scrooge used every ounce of his being to be as convincingly merciless as he could. Whether the situation could ever get as bad as he was describing was irrelevant. He knew he was such a voice of authority in the housekeeper's life that if he said it, she probably believed it was true. And she looked suitably terrified.

The butler's amused look had faded into a nervous, open mouthed stare; perhaps he was taken aback by both the sinister details of the housekeeper's behavior and the cold-hearted reaction of his employer. "Mercy, dear woman, what were you thinking?"

The housekeeper covered her face with her hands and with shoulders shaking began to cry.

Scrooge watched her cry for a moment then sensed enough was enough. He then spoke softly with words so unfamiliar to him, it couldn't have sounded more awkward if he were speaking a new language all together. "So ... I, um, forgive you." He let those words sink in before he continued. "Yes, I think if you will start anew ... that is, turnover a new leaf, I'll make you a gift of half of the money you've stolen. Give the other half to the butler, but half is for you."

The housekeeper gasped loudly. "How can you forgive?"

Seeing that the housekeeper was not stepping forward to take the money that Scrooge was holding, the butler stepped forward and did the honors of taking the money and splitting it per Scrooge's instructions. Scrooge continued in almost a whisper, but with conviction, "You see, I have it on good authority that God exists and has forgiven me because of Jesus Christ." Then as tears welled in his eyes, he continued, "He paid for my crimes. If that's true, then I suppose the least I can do is forgive you for yours. Consider yourself forgiven ... for Jesus' sake."

The housekeeper had a look of utter shock that faded to relief.

The butler looked amazed as well. He mumbled, "Did the world's most famous atheist just invoke Jesus?

There was a long, awkward pause. Then Scrooge concluded with a smile, "That's how I roll."

The housekeeper and the butler made their way toward the door together. But the housekeeper, not ready to accept the gift, paused near the dresser and placed the money back inside it. Regardless of the impact to the housekeeper and butler, Scrooge felt satisfied – surprisingly so … and more than satisfied. He felt joy, and he felt alive. Now, many people use the words joy and alive at the drop of a hat, but what Scrooge meant by those words were a feeling that no other experience in his life to that point could match. Could this have been what Fred had alluded to earlier – that he felt great joy in serving his Creator? His show of mercy to the maid had initially only been motivated by a feeling that he ought to do it. The feeling of joy had not been sought, and it had taken him by surprise. He could not know whether the housekeeper would soon forget the mercy she had been shown and the punishment she had been spared. He also could not know if she would attribute his actions to the grace of God, as he had suggested she should, or merely to some post-trauma lunacy on his part. What he did know was that he had been on the brink of death, in the very hand of the specter, but now was alive again. Every ounce of him wanted to change for the better. And with the first awkward steps of a baby learning to walk, the change was beginning.

As Scrooge lay there alone, he thought, "Why am I alive? Marley said it was my time. This can't be right. But what was it that he told me? In a time of trouble, God's light becomes like a lighthouse in a storm and that I've been sitting with my foolish back to the light.' Well, I daresay God has me quite turned around now."

Scrooge felt quite thankful for all his trouble, as strange as that may sound, and for the changes his difficulties had brought about in him. He now began the long but joyful journey of reconsidering everything he had ever assumed about the world with his new understanding of his place in the world as a servant of his Creator.

"What else did Marley tell me? 'God is not obliged to overwhelm you with the reality of his existence. Neither is he obliged to fix your health problems. Both your knowledge and your health are completely gifts from Him and you have no claim to them. Consider, though, that God has not hidden Himself from us, but instead it is we who ran away from Him.' I see now that this was all true, but I run no more.

"Oh, Jacob Marley, thank you for your service to me. God and heaven be praised."[82]

Scrooge's mind wandered back to the comment his butler had made about a woman visitor who helped save his life. The doctor had also told him that "a friend" had come to his rescue. Scrooge called for his butler, who quickly popped back in.

"Now, what was all this about a woman who visited me last night?" asked Scrooge with a zeal that could still be mistaken for sternness, even in the transformed Scrooge.

"Well, she was a lovely woman," began the butler. "She said she was looking for her son who had gone missing. She asked me if you'd seen him earlier that day. I had just gone to check on you as a result of her visit and that's when I found you ... on the floor."

"And what was her name? Did you get her name by chance?" asked Scrooge eagerly.

"Of course, sir. I wrote her name down right here, in case you wanted to thank her." said the butler, pulling a piece of paper out of his pocket. "Emily Cratchit was her name."

"I thought so. Has the boy been found?"

"I couldn't say, sir."

"Could you follow up and let me know what you find out?"

"Certainly, sir."

"I agree with you, though – a thank you should be sent ... No, on second thought, that's all right. I have other business with her tomorrow. I'll thank her in person."

Although he still felt a little tired and Christmas Day was

nearly spent, there was one other thing Scrooge felt he must not miss out on. Once the butler had called the police and confirmed that Emily's son had returned home, Scrooge asked his butler to take him to Fred's house.

The butler dropped him just outside his nephew's front door. A nervous Scrooge slowly walked from the curb to the front door. Once at the front door he resolved to knock at least a dozen times, before he had the courage to do it. But finally he did it.

"Why, bless my soul!" cried Fred. "Who's that?"

"It's your Uncle Scrooge. I have come to dinner. Will you let me in, Fred?"

Let him in! It is a mercy he didn't shake his arm off. Scrooge was at home in five minutes. Nothing could be heartier. His niece looked just the same as he had seen her in the shadow of Christmas Present. So did Topper when he came. So did everyone when they came. Wonderful party, wonderful games, wonderful unanimity, won-der-ful happiness![83]

After the group played their merry games, everyone quieted down. It was at this time that Fred inquired of the party, "Does anyone know a joke to share?"

Just as before, Topper entertained the group with his toilet paper joke, then other jokes were shared. At just the pivotal moment when Fred would have otherwise offered his joke, Scrooge shouted out, "Oh, have you ever heard the joke about the four men on an airplane?" No one had, except Fred, who said nothing but looked astonished at the coincidence that he had thought of the same joke at the same moment but dared not tell it in his uncle's presence.

So Scrooge began to tell it in earnest. "Well, there were four men on a plane – the pilot, a mountain climber, a pastor, and … me, an arrogant and stubborn atheist professor."

The self-deprecating reference brought surprised smiles to all in the group. Some thought of saying the socially polite thing, like "Oh, you're not so arrogant." But none spoke, because none could be party to a lie of such enormous magnitude.

Scrooge completed the joke, telling it just as it was supposed to be told, including his fatal mistake of jumping from the plane with only a mountain climber's backpack. And when the joke was through, he laughed harder than anyone telling a joke has a right to. After all, a joke is told for the presumed amusement of the listener, not the teller. But it was a splendid laugh, a most illustrious laugh. The father of a long, long line of brilliant laughs![84] The others responded to Scrooge's self-indulgent laughter with a strange look or two, but in a good-natured way. They were astonished, but even more so they were thrilled – both with the joke and the apparent transformation of the man they used to love to hate.

After the group was beginning to break up for the evening, Fred pulled his uncle aside and made bold to ask, "Why did you tell that joke, uncle? Why is it suddenly so funny to you that the atheist professor dies in an accident caused by his own arrogance?"

"Because, Fred, the atheist professor doesn't die. That's the part I haven't had a chance to mention yet. For some mysterious reason ... God stepped in. He pulled the falling, helpless atheist professor up and set him safely on the ground. The atheist professor had his eyes opened. Fred, can you believe it?" Scrooge continued in a hushed voice, "The atheist professor is an atheist no more." Fred looked confused, so Scrooge confessed outright, "I had a heart attack last night. I nearly died – indeed, I should have died."

"Oh, Uncle Scrooge, I'm sorry to hear of your trouble, and I'm glad you're alive and all right. And I'm thrilled beyond words to hear you say you're no longer an atheist – if you're being serious."

"Serious as a – er, well."

"But I must say, I never thought you would come to God in the way you're describing. You were scared into belief, such a rational old man as yourself? I think it's great, don't get me wrong, but I never thought it would happen like this."

"Scared into belief? No, not quite, my dear nephew. It is far more complicated than you can imagine, but suffice it to say the experience was intense enough to finally get this old man's attention and focus my thoughts to consider the question of God's existence more carefully. Rest assured that the stones you threw in my shoe were part of the whole process. 'Why does something exist, rather than nothing?' It's a good question, my nephew, and I needed to consider it.

But let me tell you what my change of heart is not. It is not a fear-based response to a near-death experience, the hedging of bets like Pascal's wager, or a blind leap of faith. It is a faith in the existence of God backed up by reason – a reasonable faith."

"And glad I am to hear it. Of course, I must ask what's next?"

Scrooge smiled and quietly took Fred into his confidence as far as he dared at the moment.

***

The next day, Scrooge set to work dealing with more serious matters than telling jokes at Christmas parties. There was a law that needed to be changed and an innocent man that needed to be saved from prison. Once at his office, he asked his assistant to arrange a meeting with Mrs. Emily Cratchit, and later that day, Scrooge was at the front door of the Cratchit home, speaking with Emily Cratchit face to face for the first time.

"Mrs. Cratchit," he began, "before I say anything else, I simply must say thank you for saving my life. I have never experienced such a benevolent act from another human being in all my life."

"You're welcome," Emily responded in a cautious, measured tone, not sure what to say. There was still a very big part of her that wished she had let him die, but she would not let herself say it.

Scrooge had hoped to be invited into the home for the duration of the conversation, but Emily had made no such gesture, so he continued. "The next thing I must do is apologize for the terrible trouble I've caused you and your husband."

"And the children no less!" added Emily who lost her control momentarily. "You have no idea –" Then she caught herself and stopped.

"Yes, the children, the children, too, and I'm so, so sorry,"

Scrooge agreed. "I know it will be difficult to believe, but I'm not the man I was, even one day ago, and I'm not the man now that I intend to be in the future. What I'm trying to say is that I have very good intentions to right the wrongs that I've done, not only against you but against all those I've harmed. I don't know if you can believe me, but I could not be more sincere. I only ask that you give me the opportunity to prove my good intentions are real."

"Well, if you're sincere, then get rid of this law you helped create and keep my husband out of prison."

"I have a plan to do just that. May I come inside to explain? It's rather hush-hush at the moment."

Emily nodded slowly and reluctantly let Scrooge into her house. She called for Bob to join her and Scrooge in the family room. Scrooge looked around the family room, recognizing the couch from his earlier visit where he and the Ghost of Christmas Present had observed Emily and Bob having their conversation just past midnight on Christmas morning. Feeling at home, Scrooge began to explain his plans for making good on his promises to Emily – how he would work to repeal the law and how to ensure her husband, under any circumstances, would stay out of prison. Both Bob and Emily thought the plans were outrageous, but to Scrooge's surprise, they agreed to play their parts.

Before their meeting ended Scrooge reached into his coat pocket and pulled out a check. "I know of one more terrible problem that I'm not actually the cause of but that I intend to fix."

"What's that?" Emily asked, looking at the check.

"It's the financial means you'll need in order to get Tim treated for a very serious problem with his leg."

Emily looked confused, but then Bob remembered how Tim had complained of leg pain for the first time ever when he got out of bed for their late night adventure to "save Santa." "How did you know he was having leg pain?" Bob asked. "I just found out myself yesterday."

"You'll find it difficult to believe, I'm afraid, so please just take my check and have him tested today, and whatever the problem is, get it treated. There's sufficient funds here to take extreme measures if necessary – just promise me you'll take action now."

"This is all very strange, but thank you. We will get him tested," Bob declared solemnly.

Later that morning, Emily and Tim left for the hospital for testing. It was about a week later when they got the news that there was a cancerous tumor on Tim's bone near his knee, not much more than 1 millimeter in diameter – so small that there was a strong chance the biopsy had taken out all of the cancerous tissue at once. While cancer is never good news, the doctors said it was detected so very early that Tim's predicted survival rate was nearly 100%. Both Bob and Emily were home when Bob got the call from the doctor. Bob squeezed Emily's hand, thanked God for prompting Scrooge to act long before they could have seen past all their other problems to discover Tim's.

***

Meanwhile, with the LWLs beginning to make good on their threat to picket the church, Bob spoke with Fred about Scrooge's plan to keep Bob out of jail and repeal the hate speech law. Fred eagerly agreed to help and spoke in turn to Topper. Topper loved the idea (which made the others nervous) and agreed to help as well. Thus a secret alliance was formed. All that remained was to put that plan into action.

A few days later, Fred and Topper arrived at Scrooge's home just before dawn. Once Scrooge had joined them they drove to a residential street about a mile from the church. Fred made a protest sign that read, "Take love to the limit, then keep going." It was not a terribly clever sign, but it would serve him just fine as he and Topper set out to impersonate Love Without Limits activists. To help conceal their identities as they mingled with the protestors, they wore disguises. Fred wore a fake beard and a bandana on his head. Topper had dyed his hair blond the night before, wore a fake handlebar mustache and a pair of sunglasses. Later that morning when the LWL activist protestors arrived to picket, Fred and Topper walked the few blocks back to the church to join them.

They could see several Love Without Limits activists protesting in the parking lot. Some had signs; some were waving at cars; and all were protesting the church and its notorious pastor. They approached the protestors and began to mingle and make friends, introducing themselves to the others with aliases and expressing their strong interest in helping the LWL cause. Fred also made a point to find out who was in charge. Once he was able to have a conversation with the organizer of the protest, he asked the man if he'd ever considered storming the building.

The organizer replied with a grin, "I think about it constantly. I want nothing more than to wring that bigoted pastor's neck. But breaking into the building would lead to an avalanche of bad publicity for our community. Make no mistake, there are some very angry protestors here, but the only one slated for bad publicity is the pastor, and that's the way I prefer it to stay."

Fred replied, "I'm not afraid to break in and have no reservations about giving it a try."

"That's not necessary. In fact, it sounds a little crazy. Your help holding a sign is quite enough."

This was an important point for Fred to get clarification on, since their plan involved storming the building and he did not want any "help" from other protestors that could cause more trouble than he intended. He thanked the organizer and went on his way, but when the coast was clear a few minutes later, Fred and Topper sprang into action, ignoring the advice they'd just received. They marched up to the glass front doors of the church and started to pull at them, but they were (as they hoped) locked. The protestors' attention was drawn by the noise of the doors rattling, and soon they were all watching Fred and Topper's pathetic break-in attempt. They went from door to door on the sides of the building that the protestors could see, pulling frantically at each only to find it locked – Topper hamming it up as only he could by turning the shaking of the door handles into something of a dance.

The protest organizer wondered aloud, "What are those jokers up to? I told them to leave the building alone."

When they had tried the last of the front doors, Topper turned around sheepishly and shrugged. The protestors were all watching and some laughed. Then, Fred and Topper marched off around the corner of the church out of sight. Minutes later, there came a pounding on the church doors from the inside. It was Fred and Topper, who were now inside the church somehow. They were jumping and high-fiving, obviously quite pleased with themselves. The protestors took notice and gave them a big cheer. Their crazy but resilient comrades had accomplished their goal – they had broken into the building. They disappeared from the protestors' sight again. This time they were gone for a bit longer, but when they returned they were not alone. With them was Pastor Cratchit, duct-taped to an office chair. The pastor appeared to those outside to have come out on the losing end in a short tussle with the two young men who had also apparently come armed with duct tape. The protestors could assume nothing other than that the newest protestors had decided to kidnap the pastor. And Bob had a genuinely scared look in his eye. It was a brilliant performance of feigned terror.

Upon the sight of the two with their prized quarry, the protestors cheered with excitement. In almost a mirror image Fred and Topper cheered back, jumping and smiling and laughing. Then suddenly Fred stopped and began pushing the desk chair and its occupant down the hall, disappearing out of sight of the protestors with Topper quickly following behind. At the other end of the building was the church's garage. A moment later, the garage door opened, and the church van came roaring out. The pastor, still bound and wild-eyed with terror, was visible in the back. The van honked at the protestors as it drove away.

Once out of sight of the protestors, Fred drove the van to the nearby neighborhood where Fred's car was parked with Scrooge waiting inside. Scrooge and Topper released Bob while Fred took the church van to an auto shop at the end of the street. Inside the shop, Fred, requested service on the church van. Fred paid for the service in advance with cash. He left the name of the church secretary and the number of the church office as the contact info for when the mechanics were done. This scheme allowed him to leave the church van keys with someone and ensure that it was safely returned back to the church without additional involvement from him, Scrooge, or Topper.

The four men then embarked on the hour-plus drive to Scrooge's riverfront retreat on the Potomac. Not a rustic cabin by any stretch of the imagination, the estate had every possible amenity. The prior owner of the opulent cottage had even named the property The Wartburg Castle.[85] Bob could live here in comfortable anonymity until the law was changed and his "kidnappers" released him.

As Fred drove, he glanced over and observed the concerned look on Bob's face. "Everything all right, Pastor Bob?"

"I'm wondering what will happen if you three are caught," Bob confessed. "What punishment might you face? How would this affect your families? Your good intentions could easily cause this bad situation to get even worse."

Fred thought for a moment and replied, "Oh, don't worry about us. It's a good plan, and we're not likely to get caught. Even if we do, though, we know we've done the right thing. It's an honor to have served in such a worthy cause."

"Agreed," said Topper. "Not that I have much to lose, but even if I had, I'm in it to win it."

On the way back to DC from their errand to The Wartburg, Scrooge, Fred, and Topper conspired to transport the rest of the Cratchit family to the cottage for brief visits until the law was changed. Fred was thrilled to have a chance to make good on his pledge to the pastor that he would make himself available to help any way that he could, but Scrooge never let on that he'd known about that pledge from the start thanks to the Ghost of Christmas Present. The next morning the headline read, "Protestors kidnap notorious pastor."

Scrooge's plan was very daring, and frankly, it was also very illegal. It was not, though, without precedent in history. In fact, the plan would later be compared to the friendly kidnapping of Martin Luther after his condemnation at the Diet of Worms. While Scrooge was now a new man who did not take the moral aspects of breaking the law lightly, he did search his conscience, and in his best judgment this was the right thing to do. He came to agree with what Luther had said before the Worms tribunal: "To go against one's conscience is neither safe, nor wise."

Once the pastor was safely sequestered, Scrooge set to work daily to undo the very law he had helped enact. On the surface, it was a project with no apparent path to success. Scrooge was a clever man, however, and what would have overwhelmed many lesser men was not overwhelming for him. Even so, he would in time need and receive a great deal of help in righting his wrong.

One fact that should have made things easier was that the majority of his countrymen did not approve of the restrictions on moral free speech. Scrooge had succeeded in passing the "hate speech" bill originally through the manipulation of politicians and the media, not by winning a majority consensus of the voting population. Even so, it was difficult to get the voting public to sit up and take notice that some of their freedom had actually been lost. While the supporters of the Love Without Limits had been fighting a war on moral free speech, many of those who would one day miss their right to moral free speech did not even see they were in a war or foresee that they were about to lose this right. And now that they had lost it, many were so atrophied and weak from sitting on the sidelines, watching the political process as if democracy was merely one more form of entertainment, that most efforts to take action resembled a turtle flipped over on its back, struggling without success to get back on its feet. On the face of it, the timeline for repealing the law could be years, if ever.

However, there were two factors that would ensure Scrooge's success against all odds. The first seemed quite providential. Months before Christmas, Scrooge had been invited to speak at a live nationwide television broadcast, scheduled to air just days after Bob's "kidnapping" the broadcast was intended to chronicle and celebrate the victories that had been won by the Love Without

Limits activists. The passage of the "hate speech" legislation was the crowning jewel of their achievements, and the producers intended to feature it and Scrooge prominently in the broadcast. At the time Scrooge was invited, he was still considered "safe" and firmly within the LWL camp. At the time of the live broadcast, only Fred, Topper, the Cratchits, and a few others knew of his change of heart.

Scrooge's first comments at the event were fairly generic and met with appreciative applause. "To the extent that the work of those being celebrated tonight has achieved victories in lessening unfair discrimination we should applaud and celebrate their efforts. Many well intentioned souls have labored tirelessly simply to do what they thought was the right thing." He paused to let the applause dissipate and then continued, "With that said, please listen carefully to what I'm about to say. In regards to the law I helped enact, I must confess that in hindsight it was an *abominable idea*. And as a matter of conscience I will do anything in my power to undo what I've done. Free speech, including moral free speech, is a bedrock of healthy democracy and a civil society. Regardless of the issue, only free debate can prevent tyranny. But as a result of this law, we, an otherwise free people, have now shackled ourselves with our own modern day Thought Police.

"Many blame the 'evil LWL activists' for ruining this great country. First of all, they're not evil as far as I can tell. Secondly, do you know whom I blame? I blame you. I blame me. That is to say, I blame the hapless victims of this legislation who didn't even try to stop its passage. Those who believe in free speech did not match the passion and commitment of those who declared war on it. The LWL activists did not win on the merits of their arguments. They won because the opposition failed to show up for the fight. We never fought for free speech. We never fought for freedom of conscience. We inherited it like - dare I say - a spoiled child, utterly taking it for granted, and it slipped through our fingers. Now we are on the outside looking in ... with ourselves to blame."

Scrooge had more he hoped to say, but by this time, he was

shouting just to be heard over the boos and groans from many (but not all) in the audience. Perhaps it was the memory of Topper's luck with the angry mob, but he made a judgment call to end his remarks. Without any signs of fear or panic, he walked off the stage. The producers, the live audience, and all involved were shocked and many were likely upset, but security was tight enough to control any loose cannons in the audience and the producers seemed so bewildered by the turn of events that no one even spoke a word to him as he calmly gathered his things and left the building. This providential opportunity allowed Scrooge to reach millions more when his comments went viral on the Internet, and their voices soon began to be heard in the halls of Congress. Scrooge's efforts were not in vain. The country was now beginning to awaken.

The second secret of his success was in his clever understanding of politicians. Scrooge knew that many politicians were conditioned to follow the shifting winds of public sentiment. While those finger-to-the-wind politicians had only moments ago voted one way, as soon as they got wind of political opponents getting ahead by having the opposite view, they changed their course and made plans to remove the very law they had helped put in place. Scrooge, being the person who "made the winds shift" to get the hate speech law passed, was in an excellent position to shift those winds in order to get the law repealed. He argued that including the repeal of the "hate speech" legislation as a line item in the latest piece of large legislation would satisfy their constituents and save their careers.

So in short order, the law was repealed and clemency was granted to those in violation of the law. Fred and Topper "released" Pastor Bob Cratchit from his captivity, and the shadow that foretold the pastor's imprisonment and its devastating effects did not come to pass.

It was several weeks after Christmas when Scrooge finally had a chance to take action on the last remaining issue from the night with the ghosts. It was early afternoon on a quiet Saturday when Scrooge walked from his home in the direction of the

Cratchit house. It was a crisp, cold afternoon, but the sun was bright and the sky was blue. He knocked on the front door, and before he had waited very long, Emily appeared in the doorway.

"Hello, Dr. Scrooge. It's so good to see you. Come in."

"Good afternoon, Mrs. Cratchit. Would it be all right if I spoke with Peter?"

"Sure, I'll get him."

When Peter emerged from his room with Emily standing behind him, he addressed Scrooge carefully as *Doctor* Scrooge.

"Yes," said Scrooge. "That is my name, and I fear it may not be pleasant to you.[86] If you will allow me, I'd like the opportunity both to apologize to you for my rude behavior and for treating you with anything less than total respect in our last meeting. Oh yes, and I want to thank you for the aspirin you gave me. The doctors tell me those aspirin helped to saved my life that night."

Peter shrugged modestly. "Sure. You're welcome."

"I've come here to see if you'd join me for a little discussion? I'd love to get to know you a little more and share some thinking on the question of God's existence."

"That'd be all right," Peter replied, again in a reserved tone.

"I know you're familiar with my old friend Marley, but I have a new friend of sorts, Gottfried Wilhelm Leibniz, whose thinking I'm sure you'll enjoy all the more! If my prior mistakes have been made right in your eyes, perhaps you'd honor me with the privilege of sitting down with you over some coffee this afternoon to discuss the question of God's existence?"

"I don't know who Leibniz is, but yeah, sure." Peter said politely.

"Is that all right with you, Mrs. Cratchit?" inquired Scrooge.

"It would be absolutely perfect," Emily assured him with a smile.

Well, Scrooge and Peter met that afternoon, and they met again on a regular basis thereafter. Scrooge and Peter became as close as Scrooge and Marley had ever been. Scrooge was more than a mentor to Peter; he was like a second father. Scrooge walked Peter from his doubt-filled agnosticism to belief in God's existence, and from there to belief that God raised Jesus from the dead, and finally – in one sense coming full circle to where he had been as a child just a few years earlier – to repentance and hope for eternal life through Jesus Christ.

While he had the faith of his childhood perhaps, he no longer held it with the mind of a child. It was not an easy or quick journey. It did not happen in one night as Scrooge's extraordinary journey had. Along the way, Peter tested Scrooge with a good many questions. Peter seemed to be the sort of young man who had difficulty dealing with doubt, but Scrooge mentored him patiently and answered his questions frankly. Brilliant as Scrooge was, he was not afraid of questions. In fact, one of the greatest things he taught Peter was to ask really good, nay, the most important questions, as a means of getting to the heart of the matter. In addition to the question, "Why is there something, rather than nothing?" which relates to the existence of God, Scrooge also taught Peter to ask, "How did Christianity get off the ground?" Scrooge explained to Peter, "This question relates to the resurrection of Jesus. I'd argue that since anyone claiming to be an eyewitness of the resurrection was in a position to know whether their claims were true or false, there are no good explanations why they willingly and repeatedly endured persecution and hardship, even death, for a lie; therefore, we should be open to the idea that what they reported was the truth."

Peter agreed by saying, "There's just no upside for dying for something you know is a lie, is there? You're right. The disciples probably believed that what they saw was a resurrected Jesus. People in history have died for a lie that they thought was the truth, but the eye witnesses were in a position to know firsthand whether their claims were true or false." Peter conceded the point, but on and on the questions from Peter came.

Scrooge once told Peter, "Never forget, there is doubt on both sides of the question. So merely having doubt is not warrant for unbelief. The sad truth about me as a young man is that when beset with doubts, I did not look earnestly for answers. Instead, I used my doubt as an excuse to turn my back on God and actively looked for new reasons to doubt. But the only response to doubt that does right by our conscience is to hold fast to our faith in God that is written on our hearts, then search for reasonable answers to resolve those doubts."

No, Peter did not become a nihilist. The shadows of a suicidal Peter under the tree which Scrooge foresaw did not come to pass. Instead, Peter became one of the great scholars of his day and a defender of the view that not only does God exist, but He also raised Jesus from the dead.[87]

Whenever Scrooge and Peter met to go to the coffee shop, they'd walk by the old church and the small cemetery next to it. And on each of those occasions Peter would observe Scrooge, more times than not, whistling with great skill for just that time when they were walking past the graveyard. Finally, Peter thought to ask, "Dr. Scrooge, why do you whistle past the graveyard?"

Scrooge smiled and replied, "Why do you think people whistle past the graveyard?"

"Well, because they want to drown out the thought of death because it makes them seriously uncomfortable, I guess."

"As a follower of Christ, I do not live as those who have no hope. I've got a very different reason now for whistling past the graveyard. Since Christ has conquered death, it has lost its sting. I don't need to fear it. My reason, most simply put, is joy."

***

People always had an eye on Scrooge, watching to see if his remarkable transformation was for real. Those who only came to know Scrooge after his transformation would invariably ask, "Is it true that you used to work to put Christians in jail?"

Scrooge would smile and answer modestly by quoting John Newton, "I remember two things very clearly: I am a great sinner and Christ is a great Savior."

Scrooge became as good a friend, as good a professor, and as good a man, as the good old city knew, or any other good old city, town, or borough, in the good old world. Some people laughed to see the alteration in him, but he let them laugh, and little heeded them; for he was wise enough to know that nothing ever happened on this globe for good at which some people did not have their fill of laughter in the outset. His own heart laughed: and that was quite enough for him. Did some people call him a Jesus freak? Well of course they did and he learned to wear the pejorative like a badge of honor. And it was always said of him, that he knew the reasons why he believed what he believed and he knew how to keep Christmas well, if any man alive possessed the knowledge of these two things. May that be truly said of us, and all of us![88]

EPILOGUE

As Professor Spassnicht finished typing, he slowly stood up from the desk. He seemed to take all his energy to stand. He made his way to the bathroom sink and spied himself in the mirror. So pale white it almost scared him. Maybe he had pushed himself a bit hard to finish the manuscript. His thoughts were interrupted by the ringing of the phone. He looked at the caller ID -- it was the Crandall residence. Spassnicht had forgotten to call Erin back as he had promised and days had passed. He quickly answered the phone.

The caller was Erin's husband Brant this time. "Edward, Erin told me about the aneurysm and that you're having surgery soon. I hope I'm not disturbing you, but I wanted to let you know that I'm very concerned."

"I'm good as gold and better, Brant," Spassnicht replied.

"You may not be concerned about your health, but let us be concerned for you."

"Oh, I'm concerned all right." Spassnicht confessed while taking a seat. "I just refuse to fret about something that I don't feel I have any control over. Regardless, I'm glad you called. I want Erin's and your help with something. I've decided to share the story of what happened that night five years ago. I know that I might not survive the operation, so I want to make sure the story is safe with someone. Would either of you be willing to take my story to the world if something happens to me?"

"If something happens to you, then Erin will just have to save your life again!" When Spassnicht laughed, Brant continued, "You're good as gold, just like you said, but if you're finally ready to share your story, we're elated and we'd be honored to help anyway we can. What made you change your mind?"

"I've not been shy about sharing my faith from the beginning and I've known that the right thing to do was to share the story, but I always feared my enemies would use the hard-to-believe aspects of the story to try to discredit me. But I feel that I've solved that dilemma – it occurred to me that I could still accomplish what was needed even if the story were written as fiction. I've just finished typing it up. I'll email it to you shortly, definitely before the surgery. Does that sound OK?"

"That's brilliant. Erin and I are done bugging you then. We'll leave you alone and we'll see you at the hospital. Let us know if you need anything and take care."

The next morning, after an egg and some tea, he sat down to reread what he had written. The professor had worked at a manic pace for several days leading up to the day of his surgery, forgoing visitors, email, and all distractions. He had typed at the speed of thought, and his first thoughts were nearly letter perfect. Spassnicht was a real genius, but in all his life he had never written so much so fast. The only thing that had slowed him was the lingering doubt about how the story would be received by his critics. But no sooner would the doubt arise when the thought of dying would overwhelm the doubt and steel his resolve to finish. His surgery was tomorrow, so he had just enough time to complete a proofreading and make a few edits. That evening he emailed it off to the Crandalls so that they could proofread and take the next steps to get it published should the worst come to pass. Retiring for the night to his bedroom, he said his prayers as usual, and laid down his head to sleep. Just before sleep overtook him, or maybe a moment after, he heard a familiar voice, a voice which declared, "It's your time, old friend."

Jeremiah 29:13

"You will seek me and find me when you search for me with all your heart."

INDEX OF TOPICS

Additional resources:

1. *Tactics* by Greg Koukl

2. *The Faith of Christopher Hitchens* by Larry Taunton

Tolerance / Moral Free Speech: Pages 71, 79, 94, 149

Additional resources: Reasonable Faith website: Question of the Week #148, http://www.reasonablefaith.org/atheist-arguments-to-in-intellectual-neutral

The Duty of Conscience: Pages 96, 147, 152

Additional resources:

1. *Martin Luther: A Man Who Changed the World* by Dr. Paul Maier (children's book, but OK for you and me too)
2. *Bonhoeffer: Pastor, Martyr, Prophet, Spy* by Eric Metaxas
3. *The Cost of Discipleship* by Dietrich Bonhoeffer

Dealing with Doubt: Pages 20, 115, 118, 123, 152

Additional Resources:

1. Reasonable Faith website: Question of the Week #29, http://www.reasonablefaith.org/site/News2?page=NewsArticle&id=5889

2. Reasonable Faith website: Question of the Week #4 http://www.reasonablefaith.org/site/News2?page=NewsArticle&id=5617

3. "Why I'm A Christian" speech by John Lennox

4. *The Reason for God* by Timothy Keller

5. *Is God Just A Human Invention?* by Sean McDowell and Jonathan Morrow

Is God Just?: Page 50, 116, 116, 118,

Additional resources:

1. *Is God a Moral Monster?* by Paul Copan
2. https://soundcloud.com/jesusisgod316/michael-ramsden-god-of-love

Arguments for the Existence of God: Page 25, 53, 108, 120

Additional Resources:

1. *Alvin Plantinga's 2 dozen (or so) arguments for God's existence:*
   http://philofreligion.homestead.com/files/theisticarguments.html

2. *Peter Kreeft Lists 20 Arguments for God's Existence:*

   http://www.peterkreeft.com/topics-more/20_arguments-gods-existence.htm

Kalam Cosmological Argument:

1. *On Guard* by William Lane Craig, Chapter 4

2. *TrueU: Does God Exist?* DVD by Focus on the Family

The Moral Argument:

1. *Mere Christianity* by C.S. Lewis, Book I

2. *On Guard* by William Lane Craig, Chapter 6

3. *TrueU: Does God Exist?* DVD by Focus on the Family

4. *Can Man Live Without God?* by Ravi Zacharias

The Argument from the Fine-Tuning of the Universe:

1. *On Guard* by William Lane Craig, Chapter 5

2. *TrueU: Does God Exist?* DVD by Focus on the Family

The Argument from the Origin of Information in the First Living Organisms:

1. *TrueU: Does God Exist?* DVD by Focus on the Family

2. *Signature in the Cell* by Dr. Stephen Meyer

The Argument from Irreducible Complexity in Biology:

1. *TrueU: Does God Exist?* DVD by Focus on the Family

2. *Darwin's Black Box* by Dr. Michael Behe

The Transcendental Argument:

J. Warner Wallace's Cold Case Christianity website: http://coldcasechristianity.com/2014/is-god-real-the-case-from-the-transcendent-laws-of-logic/

The Argument from True Miracles including the Resurrection of Jesus of Nazareth:

1. *On Guard* by William Lane Craig, Chapters 8, 9, 10

2. *The Case for the Resurrection of Jesus Christ* by Gary Habermas and Michael Licona

The Argument from Human Desire:

Peter Kreeft's website: www.peterkreeft.com/topics/desire.htm

ABOUT THE AUTHOR AND STORY

My hometown of Frankenmuth, Michigan has a history that is significant to me. It was a town settled by immigrants whose aim was to share with the native Chippewa "how beautiful it is to live with Jesus." The altruistic, missionary zeal of the town's founders inspires me and is in part the inspiration for attempting a project of this sort. Additionally, the writing of this story was influenced by the likes of C.S. Lewis, William Lane Craig, and Paul L. Maier, and through the vivid everyday witness of my family and friends. Through them, I have seen the beauty – of both the heart and mind – of a life lived with Jesus.

NOTES

[1] Charles Dickens, *A Christmas Carol*

[2] G.K. Chesterton

[3] Paraphrase of a story told on John Lennox's, "Why I'm a Christian" talk. He said it when a journalist asked him to respond to the statement from Stephen Hawking. He expressly asked if they wanted a similar soundbite from him and they confirmed that they did. So it is not meant to be a point that is too serious, but is just a parody of this kind of Freudian soundbite. John Lennox points out that neither statement proves anything either way.

[4] Charles Dickens, *A Christmas Carol*

[5] Charles Dickens, *A Christmas Carol*

[6] G. K. Chesterton paraphrase

[7] Related to the Leibnizian cosmological argument. Leibniz proposed that the first and most fundamental question a person should ask is "Why is there something, rather than nothing?" Leibniz's cosmological argument to be discussed in depth, later in the story.

[8] Blaise Pascal (*Pensées*)

[9] Charles Dickens, *A Christmas Carol*

[10] Charles Dickens, *A Christmas Carol*

[11] Charles Dickens, *A Christmas Carol*

[12] Charles Dickens, *A Christmas Carol*

[13] Charles Dickens, *A Christmas Carol*

[14] Charles Dickens, *A Christmas Carol*

[15] Charles Dickens, *A Christmas Carol*

[16] Charles Dickens, *A Christmas Carol*

[17] Charles Dickens, *A Christmas Carol*

[18] Charles Dickens, *A Christmas Carol*

[19] Charles Dickens, *A Christmas Carol*

[20] Charles Dickens, *A Christmas Carol*

[21] Charles Dickens, *A Christmas Carol*

[22] Charles Dickens, *A Christmas Carol*

[23] Paraphrase of Karl Marx

[24] "Quod est demonstrativ" is Latin for "thus it is demonstrated"

[25] Michael Ramsden, *Let My People Think* podcast

[26] Source of quote unknown. Often misattributed to C.S. Lewis

[27] Paraphrase of Ravi Zacharias, *Can Man Live Without God?*, p. 182

[28] Michael Ramsden, *Let My People Think* podcast

[29] Charles Dickens, A Christmas Carol

[30] Charles Dickens, A Christmas Carol

[31] Charles Dickens, A Christmas Carol

[32] Charles Dickens, A Christmas Carol

[33] Kristallnacht or "the Night of Broken Glass," which occurred on November 9, 1938, was one of Hitler's most infamous acts of ruthlessness against the Jews and his political enemies up to that time and is considered a turning point in Nazi strategy. The success of Kristallnacht is considered a factor in emboldening Hitler to finally pursue his "final solution." Hitler up to that point primarily used legislation to economically and politically weaken his enemies and to silence their voice. Once his enemies had been weakened by legislation, his tactic could change to employ the unbridled aggression of the Übermensch.

[34] Romans 3:23 (NIV)

[35] Romans 5:8 (NIV)

[36] Source unknown, possibly Billy Sunday or G.K. Chesterton

[37] G.K. Chesterton

[38] 1984, George Orwell

[39] Charles Dickens, A Christmas Carol
[40] Dostoevsky, "The Brothers Karamazov"
[41] Charles Dickens, A Christmas Carol
[42] The Truth Project, Focus on the Family
[43] Charles Dickens, A Christmas Carol
[44] Charles Dickens, A Christmas Carol
[45] Charles Dickens, A Christmas Carol
[46] Charles Dickens, A Christmas Carol
[47] The above joke is an adaptation of a similar joke told by Michael Ramsden, Let My People Think podcast.
[48] Charles Dickens, A Christmas Carol
[49] Charles Dickens, A Christmas Carol
[50] John 15:13, NIV
[51] Romans 5:8, NIV
[52] Charles Dickens, A Christmas Carol
[53] Charles Dickens, A Christmas Carol
[54] Charles Dickens, A Christmas Carol
[55] Dostoevsky, "The Brothers Karamazov"
[56] 1 Thessalonians 4:13 paraphrase
[57] Friedrich Nietzsche, "The Gay Science." This famous quote is from atheist philosopher, Friedrich Nietzsche. Nietzsche was considered one of the few atheist philosophers who lived relatively consistent with the atheist worldview. Namely, he embraced nihilism, moral relativism, and ultimately madness.
[58] Paraphrase from On Guard, by William Lane Craig, Chapter 2: What Difference Does It Make If God Exists? Exact quote from On Guard: And the universe, too, faces a death of its own. … There will be no light; there will be no heat; there will be no life … This is not science fiction. This is really going to happen, unless God intervenes.
[59] Kenneth Samples from Stand to Reason interview
[60] Poem was based on the argument known as "Pascal's Wager" from Pensées by Blaise Pascal
[61] Friedrich Nietzsche, "The Gay Science"
[62] Leibnizian Cosmological argument, On Guard by William Lane Craig, Chapter 3: Why Does Anything At All Exist?
[63] Leibniz was not exactly a crank theologian. He was one of the greatest mathematicians in all of history and the co-inventor of the infinitesimal calculus. William Lane Craig, "On Guard" p.54
[64] For further clarification on the insufficiency of an infinite regress of explanations to explain the universe, see William Lane Craig's website, ReasonableFaith.org, and look up the Question of the Week #248. That question was submitted to Dr. Craig by the author.
[65] A paraphrase of a quote from William Lane Craig's book, On Guard: "To claim that something can come into being from nothing is worse than magic. When a magician pulls a rabbit out of a hat, at least you've got the magician, not to mention the hat!"
[66] The illustration of the two scientists walking in the woods is adapted from a story told by William Lane Craig in his Defenders podcast.
[67] How does the need for an explanation to the universe apply to doing good science? In a nutshell, it doesn't. It is true that any explanation that transcends the physical universe is no longer in the purview of science. Science may give us clues about the explanation for the universe, but is not the right tool to provide the answer itself. Instead, it is the domain of philosophy or more specifically metaphysics to provide possible explanations. The point in the poem still stands though since all that is being claimed is that without exception good science requires that we demand explanations. While the principle that we should demand

explanations applies to science, it also surely transcends science. When science is no longer the best tool for finding the explanation we cannot simply dismiss the principle like a taxi cab. We need to "keep riding" the principle (and search for explanations) no matter where it leads.

[68] Revelations 4:11, KJV: "Thou art worthy, O Lord, to receive glory and honor and power: for thou hast created all things, and for thy pleasure they are and were created."

[69] C.S. Lewis used a "Lord, liar, lunatic" trilemma approach for responding to the claim that Jesus was merely a great moral teacher in Mere Christianity.

[70] Dr. William Lane Craig, On Guard

[71] Dr. William Lane Craig, On Guard

[72] Dr. Stephen Meyer, Signature in the Cell

[73] Dr. William Lane Craig, On Guard

[74] Dr. Stephen Meyer, True U DVD: Does God Exist?

[75] www.pleaseconvinceme.com

[76] Dr. William Lane Craig, On Guard

[77] Dr. Peter Kreeft develops this argument on his website. Based in part on a C.S. Lewis quote from Mere Christianity. http://www.peterkreeft.com/topics/desire.htm

[78] Dr. Alvin Plantinga's 2 dozen (or so) arguments for the existence of God: http://philofreligion.homestead.com/files/theisticarguments.html

[79] William Lane Craig, On Guard or Philosophical Foundations for a Christian Worldview

[80] Charles Dickens, A Christmas Carol

[81] Paraphrase of Jeremiah 29:13

[82] Charles Dickens, A Christmas Carol

[83] Charles Dickens, A Christmas Carol

[84] Charles Dickens, A Christmas Carol

[85] Martin Luther was the subject of a "friendly kidnapping" by a group under the orders of a regional ruler, known as Frederick the Wise, whose goal was to protect Luther from those who would kill him for taking a stand against the corruption in the church of that day. The successful strategy they employed after the kidnapping was to hide Luther in the Wartburg Castle in Germany. Luther was eventually able to return to public life, continuing his reform of the church and never recanting the views that had put him in danger. Luther eventually died of natural causes, not at the hands of his enemies.

[86] Charles Dickens, A Christmas Carol

[87] This mentoring relationship is not unlike the relationship between Dr. Gary Habermas and Dr. Michael Licona who eventually co-authored the highly acclaimed book, "The Case for the Resurrection of Jesus Christ"

[88] Charles Dickens, A Christmas Carol

Made in the USA
Lexington, KY
27 September 2018